Praise for
MENACING GROVES

"A sophisticated, well-written British-style mystery."
Houston Chronicle

"The solution is unusual and unexpected, but perfectly logical. Good story."
The Chattanooga Times

"A tour de force, if you will pardon the pun... [Sherwood's] heroine, the bright and charming lady of a certain age, Celia Grant, is caught up by a murder in Italy.... Here is a trans-Atlantic Mrs. Pollifax for all seasons."
The Courier-Gazette

"John Sherwood is a good plot-spinner. Celia Grant is a delightful detective."
The Muncie Star

"Delightful... Sherwood's witty entertainment is garnished with descriptions of romantic Italian edens and of the eccentrics among Celia's traveling companions."
Publishers Weekly

Also by John Sherwood
Published by Ballantine Books:

FLOWERS OF EVIL
THE MANTRAP GARDEN
A BOTANIST AT BAY
GREEN TRIGGER FINGERS

MENACING GROVES

John Sherwood

BALLANTINE BOOKS • NEW YORK

Library of Congress Catalog Card Number: 88-18442

ISBN 0-345-35975-5

This edition published by arrangement with Charles Scribner's Sons, an Imprint of Macmillan Publishing Company.

Manufactured in the United States of America

First Ballantine Books Edition: July 1990

❦ PROLOGUE ❦

"We shall be here all night at this rate," said Celia Grant gloomily. "It's after ten and Ophelia has yet to go mad."

It was a fine summer evening in Sussex. The interval had been reached at last in the middle of an eccentric avant-garde production of Shakespeare's *Hamlet*, which was being given in the garden of a second-rank stately home as part of a local Arts Festival organized with more enthusiasm than expertise. The tyrannical young producer had insisted on performing the enormously long text uncut.

Celia's Uncle Hugo, whose guest she was, shifted uncomfortably in his seat. "I would like," he quoted, " 'to sleep, perchance to dream.' But the chairs are too hard and the insects too voracious."

"No one could sleep through all this carry-on and screaming," Celia pointed out.

"The producer must be a maniac," said Sir Hugo. "Can he really believe that Hamlet's basic trouble was a guilty passion for Horatio?"

Celia studied her programme. " 'Percival Tench's aim in producing the play,' " she read, " 'has been to let the full text make its impact, uncluttered with conventional interpretations from the past.' I suppose that's why he's given

1

Hamlet and Horatio punk hair-dos, but why are most of the others in eighteenth-century wigs?''

"To widen the generation gap, I imagine," said Sir Hugo, and rose from his hard chair. "This calls for decisive action, one of us must be suddenly taken ill so that we can go home."

"Oh dear, if only we could."

"We can. I sat through interminable tribal dances in the course of my ambassadorial duties, but I see no reason why, at the age of seventy-two, I should sit through any more of this."

Celia listened to the roar of engines from the car park. "A lot of people seem to have reached the same conclusion. You go, I can't."

"Why not, my dear?"

"You forget. I've promised to give those two actors a lift afterwards. The couple with the handicapped child who are staying with the Claytons."

The festival was being run on a shoestring. To keep costs down the artists were being given hospitality in the surrounding villages, and transport to and from rehearsals and performances. Fortunately Sir Hugo, arriving from the opposite direction to Celia, had come in his own car.

"My poor Celia, must I really leave you to the tender mercies of Percival Tench and his posturing lunatics?"

"I shall survive. I shall think beautiful thoughts and pretend it isn't happening, like a Buddhist."

Muttering more apologies, he went, and Celia settled down amid a much depleted audience to endure the remainder of the performance.

Having "done" *Hamlet* at school she knew it well, and soon realized that the actors, alarmed by the lateness of the hour, were cutting their lines drastically as they went along. King Claudius shortened his long prayer to be forgiven for murdering his brother, and Hamlet, upbraiding his mother Queen Gertrude in the closet scene, broke off his reproaches without warning in mid-tirade. But she seemed not to have expected this. A long silence followed. By the time she cried dramatically: "Oh Hamlet! Speak no more!" the remark had become unnecessary.

Laughter broke out in the sparse ranks of the audience. From then on, the performance went rapidly downhill, as if the actors' only concern was to get it over as quickly as possible. Hamlet's departure for England was left out altogether, Rosencrantz and Guildenstern were hurried on and off the stage with little or nothing to say for themselves, and the graveyard scene with Yorick's skull was reduced to a few brief exchanges. Much sooner than she dared to hope, Celia was able to go into the house to collect Polonius and Queen Gertrude, the couple whom she was to take back to their hosts' house on her way home.

She left them time to change, then went to the library, which the cast were using as a greenroom. The door was open and she walked in, but no one noticed her. They were busy with a furious post-mortem on the performance, and voices were raised in anger.

"Look Perce, we'd have been OK if Old Mother Hubbard here hadn't got that laugh," said Horatio, still in his punk hair-do. "One laugh like that against the show, and we'd lost the audience for good."

"Yes, Perce," Hamlet chimed in. "That was what threw us, her standing there for hours like the Statue of Liberty before she took her cue."

"You didn't give me a cue, you snotty-nosed little mass of arrogance," retorted Queen Gertrude.

Polonius laid a worried hand on her arm, but she shook him off. "I warned you, Perce. I told you it would play too long, but oh no, you were too busy being a boy genius to use a stop-watch at rehearsals."

Percival Tench rounded on Polonius. "For God's sake keep your shrew of a wife in order and out of my hair."

"You two old miseries make me vomit," said Ophelia in silvery tones.

"You make us all vomit." Perce turned to the others. "Don't they?"

There were savage shouts of agreement, and Celia decided that this bullying had gone on for long enough. "When you're ready, Mr. Vincent," she interrupted, "I'm here to take you and Mrs. Vincent home."

Everyone turned to look. In the presence of a member of the public the angry voices were hushed and the Percival Tench Company became a brotherhood of sweetness and light. Public relations had set in.

"Oh yes, how kind," said Polonius. "We'll go and get our coats."

Waiting for them in the corridor, Celia decided that she was very sorry for the Vincents. They were the oldsters in an otherwise young cast, and they had been made the scapegoats for the evening's fiasco. They were very bad actors, and would have trouble finding work elsewhere if they lost what seemed to be a precarious foothold in this far from prosperous theatrical troupe. Moreover they had a Down's syndrome child to support, one of the handicapped children who in an unkinder age were called mongols. No wonder Polonius had been worried by his wife's outburst. They could not afford to be too rude to Percival Tench.

On the way in the car Mrs. Vincent invited Celia to call them Jimmy and Paula, and went on to unload much venomous theatrical gossip. Ophelia, she said, would "climb into bed with a crocodile if it would help her career". The camp on-stage love affair between Hamlet and Horatio was a pale imitation of what happened off it. The salaries were miserable and irregularly paid, and Percival's grim Marxist production of Noel Coward's *Hay Fever* had been hissed off the stage in Huddersfield. All this lasted till Celia pulled into the drive to drop them at their destination, the Claytons' farm.

The Claytons had had a Down's syndrome child themselves. Since it died, they continued to give support to families with the same affliction, and this was why they had offered hospitality to the Vincents and their son during the festival. "They're darling people, so kind," said Paula Vincent. "It's black misery putting Tom in a home when we're working. He hates it and so do we."

The front door opened. Rhona Clayton came out in her dressing-gown looking harassed, and reported that the child had refused to settle down in the strange surroundings. After grizzling and fretting all evening, he had worked himself up into a hysterical state. Only his parents could calm him. Would they go upstairs at once?

The child's screams could be heard in the drive, and Jimmy Vincent rounded on his wife. "You see, Paula? Why must you drag him round with us? This always happens."

Ignoring him, Paula dashed into the house.

"Why the hell can't you leave him in the home?" Jimmy shouted after her. Then, with a hasty word of thanks to Celia for the lift, he vanished indoors.

Celia drove on to her cottage at Archerscroft Nurseries. Exhausted by her overdose of inferior Shakespeare and tiresome theatrical behavior, she went straight to bed without garaging her car, and it was not till she came out before breakfast to do some watering in the frame-yard that she noticed Paula Vincent's handbag lying on the back seat.

A nuisance. But she had a huge order of Korean chrysanthemums to dispatch by rail. Bill Wilkins, her head gardener, could drop it off at the Claytons' when he went to the station in the van.

She found him collecting seed from the semi-double primroses, one of the Archerscroft specialities. "Oh, Celia, could you go?" he begged. "I got this to do, Harry's sick and that new girl in the dispatch shed didn't turn up this morning."

Celia knew only too well why the new girl in the dispatch shed had absented herself. Bill was young and well-built, and his looks made impressionable young women go weak at the knees. The new girl had been making saucer eyes at him for weeks, and he had lost his temper with her. Since his steady girlfriend's death the previous year, he had become brutal to the point of sadism in the way he made it clear to weak-kneed young women that there was nothing doing.

Bill in a bad mood made Celia quake in her shoes. To placate him she took the chrysanthemums to the station herself and called in at the Claytons' on her way back, to find Rhona Clayton about to drive into the village and shop.

"Oh thanks, do take it in and give it to her," she said when Celia produced Mrs. Vincent's handbag. "And chat her up a bit if you can bear it, she seems to have worked herself up into rather a state."

"Isn't he there too?" Celia asked, not welcoming this chore.

"No, she had a row last night with the producer, and he's gone in on the bus to try to patch it up. She's convinced herself that she's got them both the sack from the company, and she thinks hubby will walk out on her to punish her."

With Bill short-handed and in a bad mood, Celia had no time to spare. "Must I, Rhona? I'm a bit rushed."

"I wish you would, because I know what it's like from when our poor little Nicky was alive. Suddenly the future would look black as ink and I'd work out frightful scenarios with the cows all getting mastitis and the house burning down."

Submitting to emotional blackmail, Celia went indoors and gave the handbag to Paula Vincent, who was sitting in the big farmhouse kitchen. There was no sign of the child.

"Where is he?" she asked.

"Asleep, dear. He had a bad night, poor lamb. If you'd like coffee, there's some on the stove."

Celia helped herself and sat down.

"I was up with him till four," Paula Vincent added. "And this morning I look like a hag from hell."

"No, no," Celia murmured.

Paula fixed her with a beady look, like the Ancient Mariner about to unleash his narrative. Celia expected a repeat performance of the saga of the lost job and the deserting husband. But no, Paula was off on a different tack.

"You wouldn't believe it to look at me now, dear, but I was a raving beauty once."

Celia made a sympathetic noise. Mentally subtracting the badly hennaed hair, she decided that the hatchet face with its prominent nose might once have been handsome in a horsefaced way, but not beautiful.

Launching into her life story, Paula explained that she and her Jimmy came from South Africa. "I know that makes us subhuman, but we couldn't help being born there, could we? I met Jimmy at drama school in Durban, he was a real pin-up then, and we lived together on the diciest imaginable shoestring until suddenly we started to have this raving success, playing juvenile leads in Johannesburg and Cape Town, and Jimmy thought we should get married so we did. But of course the scope's limited in South Africa, at least it was all those years ago, no television in case it gave the blacks ideas and damn little film work. Jimmy lost his head completely and had this idiotic vision of our shoes being filled with champagne and drunk out of by West End managements in London, and after a lot of argument I agreed to come. It worked OK for a bit, in provincial rep and so on. But it fizzled out quite soon, because my poor Jimmy lost his looks."

It seemed to Celia that Jimmy's blank, regular features had withstood the ravages of time better than hers, but she let that pass.

"It's awful, dear," Paula went on, "when one partner in a theatrical marriage is successful and the other isn't. I've always been able to do character parts, in fact I love them. But Jimmy can't act for toffee; he's a juvenile lead or nothing and now he's too old for it. I turned down a hell of a lot of opportunities when there wasn't a part for him, that's why I never made it to the West End."

Celia would have been hard put to it to say which of the two was the worse actor, they were both appallingly bad.

"Then of course there was the child," Paula went on. "I was too old, I should never have had one, but I'm glad I did. When your child is born and turns out to be handicapped, two things can happen. Either you say 'Take it away, it's deformed, I don't want it,' or else you say 'He's mine, he's helpless just like any other baby, except that he's going to be helpless all his life.' Jimmy didn't see it that way, he took it very badly. I think he'd have left me there and then, except that he was getting no work and I was his bread and butter. Even now we quarrel a lot about poor Tom. They're very affectionate, you know. That's why I try to bring him with us when we're working instead of dumping him in a home, he hates that. But Jimmy always kicks up a fuss when I bring him."

Was Jimmy right? The boy's distress at spending the night in strange surroundings suggested that he was.

To strike a cheerful note Celia said: "Anyway, you're both in work now."

She nodded wearily. "Perce does five or six of these crazy productions of his a year, and when he can get the finance he makes way-out films that win prizes at sleazy little festivals and make no money at all. I could do better elsewhere on my own, but I stick it out because my marriage comes first. You see, there are parts here for Jimmy."

Having satisfied her social conscience with twenty minutes worth of sympathetic noises, Celia drove crossly back to Archerscroft. Damn, she thought, I am sorry for her but why do I feel guilty about her? I suppose because one isn't allowed to dislike the mother of a handicapped child, it's as bad as disliking the Virgin Mary. Paula's affection for the child was the most genuine and likable thing about her.

Why, Celia wondered, had she been treated to this elaborate fiction, which purported to be Paula's life story? Answer, because she had been cast in the role of the stranger who can be told intimate secrets because the teller never expects to meet the hearer again. To embroider the truth in such circumstances was legitimate, but what had happened

8

to the other scenario, the tragic picture retailed to Rhona Clayton of a husband about to desert and a job about to vanish? Presenting two different pieces of embroidery to different hearers was going a bit far.

What was the unembroidered truth? Had she and Jimmy really blazed as stars in the South African theatrical sky? Did Paula really believe that Jimmy had been a drag on her career? Did Jimmy say the same thing about her, or was he better at facing the fact that they were both failures? Was it true that Jimmy had rejected their handicapped child? Perhaps he was just as fond of him as she was, but thought Tom would be happier in the stable surroundings of a home. Celia always hated not knowing the truth. In the weeks that followed, the problem of the Vincents nagged at her.

Feeling ambivalent about them made it worse. One had to be sorry for people who were reduced to working for a third-rate experimental company with a half-mad producer and a cast of arrogant young hooligans who insulted them. A bad actress with a husband who was no better, a handicapped child and an uncertain future could be excused for fantasizing a bit, but why did her fantasies have to be so bitchy? Torn between pity and dislike, Celia went on worrying about the Vincents long after they had vanished to wherever they had come from.

Damn them, she thought, I shall never see them again, so why should I let them haunt me?

But they went on haunting her, and she was destined to see them again. A year later they were to come back into her life with the devastating effect of a delayed-action bomb.

❧ ONE ❧

"On the left of the aircraft you can see Mont Blanc," said
the pilot over the intercom. Celia, who had a window seat,
stared out over the snow-covered peaks. Here she was, an
hour out from London Airport, and racked with guilt. She
was playing truant, half-way to Italy on a package tour at
Archerscroft Nurseries' busiest time of year.

This appalling dereliction of duty was the result of a phone
call a week ago from Margaret, her sister-in-law and the
head-mistress of a famous girls' school in the West Country.
Since the death of Celia's husband, Roger, they had seen
little of each other, but the phone call was an SOS. Margaret
had planned to spend the Whitsun holiday on a tour of the
historic gardens of Tuscany, organized by a small, very
exclusive travel agency. At the last minute she could not
go. Although her insurance covered cancellation in case of
illness, the death of a close relative and various other un-
foreseeable calamities, it did not cover being asked unexpectedly to chair a Royal Commission probing yet again
into the causes of juvenile crime. Was there anyone among
Celia's gardening contacts who would take her place on the
tour, and save her the annoyance of paying for a luxurious

holiday she could not have? She had tried all her own friends without success.

The tour was an interesting one, and included visits to a number of private gardens round Florence and Lucca which were not open to the public. But the cost was formidable, and there were no takers among the people Celia rang.

"You oughter go yourself," said Bill Wilkins. "Oh Celia, you should, you never got a proper holiday last winter."

"A holiday? Me? In *May*? You must be mad."

"It's only a week. Think we can't manage without you for a week? Don't be such a big-headed workaholic."

"Who'll get the copy ready for the autumn catalogue?"

"You will, before you go."

"But the trip costs the earth," she objected.

"Charge it up as a business expense. Go on, Celia, the tax man won't know different. Besides, you got a professional reason for going. You ought to see them irises in Florence."

Florence was the world centre for bearded irises, and an iris was the city's emblem. The tour was to spend an afternoon at its International Iris Competition, an annual event which attracted entries from all over the world.

"Oh Celia, how can you have the nerve to be on Floral Committee B and sit in judgment on people's irises at the Horticultural Hall when you haven't seen the Florence iris show? Ring her and say you'll go yourself in her place."

"Floral Committee B has nothing to do with irises,"* she objected. But he went on bullying her till she caved in. "And don't you go investigating no mysteries while you're away," Bill insisted. "You have a proper holiday."

So there she was, in her window seat above the Alps, agonizing about the proof-reading of the autumn catalogue

---

*Irises are judged by a joint committee of the Royal Horticultural Society and the Iris Society.

and the fate of some seedlings of *Helleborus* "Roger Grant", the *corsicus x niger* hybrid she had named in memory of her husband. There was a long waiting-list for them, and they were looking very miffy.

Sitting beside her in the plane was another threat to her peace of mind: a small, very upright man in his fifties with a pouter pigeon chest and bright, wide-open eyes, who was also bound for the historic gardens of Tuscany. He had attached himself to her in the check-in queue, asked for a seat next to hers and insisted on carrying her hand baggage to the plane as well as his own. Being small and fragile looking, with a china-doll complexion and prematurely silver hair, she was permanently at risk from men whose protective urges overcame them, as in this case. During the take-off he had plumped his hand down on hers and made reassuring remarks about how safe air travel was. "I must have covered over a million miles by air, never had a scratch."

Celia too had ranged the world's airways with Roger, having accompanied him on a dozen plant-hunting expeditions on behalf of Kew Gardens. "I'm not at all alarmed," she said coldly, and retrieved her hand. But this did not put him off.

"The name's Gatling," he told her. "But do call me Harry. I'm so glad we ran into each other, it's a bore being alone on this sort of jaunt."

Celia refrained from saying that they had not "run into each other". He had run into her like a determined little bull, and if she had not been strapped to her seat in an aircraft she would have run away at top speed from him. If he went on fawning over her ridiculously during the tour, she would have to choke him off by being very rude. Otherwise all the women would close ranks and excommunicate her as a sex-starved aging minx in search of a playmate.

Seizing on a pretext for a temporary escape, she pushed past him to make an unnecessary visit to the toilet.

And half-way down the aisle she came face to face with them: Polonius and Queen Gertrude, sitting bolt upright and looking as unreal and theatrical as ever.

No, she thought, it can't be them, it's a pair of look-alikes.

But look-alikes did not come in pairs. Artificially golden curls had replaced Queen Gertrude's depressing henna, but there was no mistaking the hatchet face with a discontented twist to the mouth. Polonius with his thinning straw-colored hair and handsome, blank features was equally unmistakable. There was no possibility of error, every detail of that disturbing encounter with them last summer was etched painfully in her mind; except, she suddenly realized, their name.

She returned to her seat and defended herself against her unwanted admirer by opening a book she had brought with her for background reading.* The opening sentence of the first chapter was a quotation from a letter written from Italy in 1596 by Sir Thomas Chaloner to the Earl of Leicester in England. "Such a rabble of English now roam Italy," he complained, and his remark applied even more forcibly now. The Poloniuses were part of the present-day rabble, Celia decided. They were bound for some overcrowded seaside resort where they would lie about like beached seals and fry themselves in smelly oil. Even if it had occurred to them to tour the historic gardens of Tuscany, they would not have been able to afford it. Being on the same flight with them was a coincidence that did not matter.

But when the plane landed at Pisa and the passengers waited for their suitcases to appear on the carousel, she found that it did matter, very much. Queen Gertrude's cabin bag bore the discreet green label of Farthingale Tours, the same as her own. The idea of sharing the historic gardens

---

*John Dixon Hunt, *Garden and Grove: The Italian Renaissance Garden in the English Imagination*: 1600–1750. London 1986.

of Tuscany with the Poloniuses filled her with irrational horror. What had they done with their Down's syndrome child? And how on earth could they afford the formidable price of the tour?

Ignoring the small talk of her admirer, she studied them more closely. Their fortunes seemed to have taken a dramatic upturn. Polonius carried an expensive video camera and the opulent message of Queen Gertrude's crocodile handbag with its gold fittings was emphasized by matching crocodile-skin shoes. The upmarket golden curls which had replaced the henna could not have been cheap, and she wore an impressive diamond ring. What had happened? How had they come by this sudden wealth?

Luggage from the flight began to arrive. "Edward, there are our cases," said Queen Gertrude in a stately voice that would have carried to the back of the upper circle.

Was he really called Edward? Perhaps, but Celia's mind was blank. Some capricious Freudian filter mechanism, which had let through a painful memory of everything else about these two, had suppressed their names. As she tried to dredge them up from her subconscious, she was attacked by an under-sized man with a self-important little beard and a woman with a green Farthingale Tours label on a dismal tapestry shoulderbag. She was looking hot in a dirndl and a rather absurd peasant straw-hat.

"How do you do? I'm Evadne Price," she said, "and this is my husband Jeremy."

"Oh. How d'you do? I'm Celia Grant."

"And this is your husband," Mrs. Price decided after a glance at Celia's wedding-ring.

"No! Mr. Gatling just happened to sit next to me on the plane."

"Major Gatling, actually," he corrected with a mock-modest smirk.

"Why are there no baggage trolleys ready for us?" demanded Mr. Price.

"It's scandalous, on an expensive tour like this," added Evadne.

Celia had been wondering about baggage trolleys. Major Gatling had attached himself to her like a determined little limpet, and unless there were trolleys he would try to carry her suitcase as well as his own out to the waiting coach, and probably both their cabin bags too.

"We shall complain," said Mr. Price, and darted off to attack the tour leader, Professor Winkworth. He was an eminent Oxford historian specializing in the Italian Renaissance, and a leading member of the Historic Gardens Society. His knowledge was immense, and so was his ability to dispense gentle old-world charm. But he had mislaid his boarding card at London Airport, and clearly did not have the practical cast of mind needed to conjure up baggage trolleys out of thin air.

After listening courteously to a long tirade from Mr. Price, he said: "Oh my dear fellow, why work yourself up into a state over a trifle? You'll enjoy the tour much more if you take life as it comes."

A porter arrived pushing a long train of baggage trolleys.

"Ah, a charioteer to the rescue," said the Professor. "Calm, masterly inactivity solves many problems, you'll find."

A coach was waiting outside the airport building, to take the party to the hotel in a spa under the foothills of the Apuan Alps which was to be its base. They were ushered into it by the courier who would deal with practical problems beneath Professor Winkworth's notice, or perhaps beyond his competence. He was a young and very good-looking Italian with greenish eyes and luxuriant dark curls. Professor Winkworth picked up the microphone beside his seat in the front of the coach and introduced him as "our friend and mentor Paolo Benedetti, who will be looking after us and keeping us in order during our daily comings and goings, and we welcome him to our company."

"Thank you, *Signor Professore*," said Paolo, taking over

15

the microphone. "I am so very happy to meet you all. And now please we go, journey time perhaps forty minutes, to your hotel in Montecatini Terme."

"Must we?" complained Mr. Price from half-way down the coach. "We are in Pisa, whose art treasures are almost as rich as those of Siena and Florence itself. Can we not enjoy them for a time before we are dragged off to this hotel?"

The Professor looked as if he might cave in before this onslaught, but Paolo dealt with it firmly. Putting on a penitent face, like a puppy being scolded for messing the carpet, he said: "I am so sorry. At the end of the tour there is arranged an afternoon free in Pisa when you can enjoy the *Triumph of Death* and the Hanging Tower and all the other touristic things. So I think it's better now if we go to the hotel."

But the Prices still nourished their grievance, and turned to grumble about it through the hole between their headrests to the couple sitting behind them. Getting only a noncommittal response, they buried their noses industriously in their Italian phrasebooks.

Celia had managed to shake off Major Gatling. But a big, heavily built man with a jolly, round face and a gingery beard had undressed her mentally through rimless glasses as they waited to board the coach. Satisfied with what he saw, he had followed her on board, taken the seat beside her and introduced himself as Nigel Monk. During the Prices' attempted revolt he put his head close to hers and murmured in her ear: "What an aggressive little man, look at the silly beard hiding the weak chin."

His own beard was too close to her for comfort, and she shrank away from it. "There's always at least one compulsive grumbler on an outing like this," he said, "and it's almost always a weedy, undersized man who's overcompensating madly."

It seemed to Celia that large men who thrust their beards into women's ears must also be compensating for some-

16

thing, but she refrained from saying so. "Do undersized women overcompensate too?" she asked.

The eyes behind the rimless glasses sparkled. "How amusing. I make a general remark, and you immediately find in it a personal application to yourself."

"No. You were putting forward a crude generalization, so I challenged you to follow it up with an even cruder one."

Her remark did not silence him as she had hoped. He treated it as the opening gambit in a flirtatious sparring match. She had exchanged the Gatling frying-pan for an equally uncomfortable fire, and found herself locked into an exchange of idiocies which lasted for the rest of the journey.

Montecatini Terme, which was to be the group's base during the tour, was an old-world spa resort overlooked by hills, with an elaborate park at its centre. The steps up to the hotel entrance were flanked by huge terracotta pots containing a stunning display of azaleas in vivid orange and reds, mostly, Celia noted with patriotic satisfaction, derivatives of Anthony Waterer's Knap Hill hybrids. Delighted by this sight, she omitted to study the suitcases as they were carried in from the coach, and discover the Poloniuses' name from their luggage labels.

Up in her room, she forced herself to take the Polonius problem seriously. What on earth was their surname, or rather surnames? For theatrical purposes they presumably had one each, but they must be travelling as Mr. and Mrs. something. Farthingale Tours had provided her with a list of the people in the party, perhaps that would jog her memory. She fished it out of her handbag and studied it.

Colonel and Mrs. E. R. Armstrong	Kent
Miss J. Armstrong	Kent
Miss J. L. M. Burton	Cheshire
Lady Carstairs	Hampshire
Mr. and Mrs. R. J. Enderby-Scott	London

Mr. K. Fanshawe	Norfolk
Miss D. R. French	Cheshire
Major H. N. Gatling	Berkshire
Miss M. C. Grant	Devon

That was a mistake, of course. The list had been typed before Celia replaced her sister-in-law at the last moment.

Mr. and Mrs. E. N. Hanson	South Africa
Mr. G. L. Johnson	Hampshire
Miss I. King	Surrey

Glancing on down to the end of the alphabet, Celia found that of the men with wives attached, only Colonel Armstrong and Mr. Hanson had the right initial, assuming that "E" for Edward could be relied on. But the Poloniuses could not possibly be a military gent from Kent with a wife and, presumably, daughter in tow, so that left only Mr. and Mrs. E. N. Hanson. Moreover South Africa was right, it was where the Poloniuses had started their acting careers.

But why did the Poloniuses describe themselves as South African now? Had they inherited money from some South African relative, settled there and come back to Europe on a visit? If so, it was quick work, less than a year ago they had been a seedy theatrical couple operating just above the breadline. In their new-found affluence they would hardly want to be reminded of that, and Celia had no intention of jogging their memory by claiming acquaintance. They had probably forgotten her anyway.

Having bathed and changed, she came downstairs and joined the crowd having pre-dinner drinks round the bar, where a quick peek as Polonius signed a chit for two gins and tonic confirmed that he and Queen Gertrude were indeed the Hansons. A little eavesdropping on the general conversation brought it home to Celia that she was surrounded by extreme wealth. Almost everyone had just been, or was just about to go, on luxurious botanical tours of Latin America or China, and almost everyone deplored the frightful nuisance of having to open one's garden to the public at intervals during the summer for charity. A lugubrious lady in black wished she did not have to dead-head a hundred yards of herbaceous border before letting the public in. A suspiciously elegant bachelor from Norfolk had had his orangery vandalized by visitors, and two women from Cheshire travelling together reported massive losses through what one of them referred to as finger blight. "People pinch off so many cuttings," she complained, "that there's nothing left of the plant."

Celia was determined to have neither Major Gatling nor Nigel Monk as her dinner neighbor. But she achieved this only at the cost of sitting opposite the mysteriously enriched Poloniuses, whom she must now think of as the Hansons. On her right she had the Armstrong family, consisting of a solid, common-sensical colonel, his artifically raven-haired wife, and a daughter whose features, dimly discernible through a mass of overhanging mousy locks, wore the discontented expression of a teenager dragged abroad by her parents against her will.

On her left was Lady Carstairs, a plump woman in her sixties, elegantly overdressed in cream-colored silk. She had a froth of fluffy white hair and a very heavy pink-and-white make-up, and reminded Celia of a huge white Persian cat with an overdose of lipstick. Beyond her was George Johnson, a loutishly handsome young man whom she introduced as her stepson.

"This is our hols, innit love?" he said as the wine waiter hovered over him. "Let's celebrate, let's 'ave some champagne, why not?"

Unease spread round the table. George had golden highlights in his hair which owed nothing to nature, and his fingers were stained with nicotine. His accent was very down-market, the culture gap between him and Lady Carstairs was enormous. Farthingale Tours digested in well-bred silence a strong suspicion that the "stepson" was a rent boy, picked up by the overdressed old lady to enliven her bedroom while on holiday.

Anxiously catering for his whim, Lady Carstairs summoned the wine waiter. But Nigel Monk leaned forward from farther down the table. "If I were you, I wouldn't waste money buying champagne, it's terribly overrated. Some of the Italian sparkling wines are far more interesting and a lot cheaper."

"Naow, let's 'ave the reel thing," George insisted.

Nigel Monk seemed to be enjoying some secret joke. "Oh please, I can't bear to see you throw your money away," he insisted, and seized the list from the wine waiter. "Bring our friends here a bottle of the Asti Spumante."

"Waiter, may I see the list?" said Lady Carstairs firmly. She ordered a bottle of Mumm, demi-sec, and froze Nigel Monk with a look, like a haughty Persian cat intimidating a dog. Mrs. Armstrong, by way of restoring public order after this tense episode, asked her opposite neighbors, a youngish, rather silent couple called Enderby-Scott, if they were keen gardeners. The question seemed to embarrass them, and they consulted each other mutely.

"We don't have a garden at the moment," said Mr. Enderby-Scott. "We're living in London."

"I wish you could see our garden outside Cape Town," said Mrs. Hanson suddenly, in the high, singing voice she used for Shakespeare's more elevated flights of poetry. "There's a wistaria pergola a hundred yards long, and the scent of the lemon trees on the evening air is like a dream. But of course it's the dead season now, we always spend it in the Bahamas, we have a house there too. We were on our way there through London when we saw about this tour and decided it would be fun, so we came."

Damn, she is fantasizing again, Celia thought. All the mixed feelings from last year flooded back: dislike, pity and deep embarrassment at a far from competent performance.

Her remarks had provoked another disapproving silence,

which Mrs. Armstrong broke by asking Celia which part of the country she came from. Celia had a moment of panic. Mrs. Hanson had been stealing glances at her across the table from time to time, as if wondering where she had seen her before. If she said "Sussex" it might open the floodgates of memory, with results too embarrassing to contemplate. But there was an obvious solution: she would step into her sister-in-law's shoes and be Miss Grant from Devon, as per the Farthingale Tours list. It would be quite safe, according to the list there was no one else from Devon in the party.

Farther down the table, Evadne and Jeremy Price craned their necks forward. "Whereabouts in Devon?"

Under duress, Celia invented a cottage for herself near Lynton, modelled on one belonging to an old school-friend she visited from time to time. But she repented of this rash fiction when it turned out that the Prices, though listed by Farthingale Tours as inhabitants of Birmingham, had a holiday cottage between Lynton and Barnstaple. It also occurred to her to wonder what she would say if someone at the table asked her why a woman calling herself Miss Grant from Devon was wearing a wedding-ring.

Back in her room, she managed with a struggle to get it off her finger, and decided to exert great strength of mind and dismiss the whole Hanson carry-on from her mind. She was on holiday. It was no business of hers, and there was nothing she could do about it. If she told Professor Winkworth that he had a pair of semi-starving actors among his flock, pretending to be stinking rich, he could only answer her with some charming old-world equivalent of "so what?" Anyway, there was probably a simple explanation; they had won two places on the tour as a prize in some breakfast food competition.

As Farthingale Tours boarded the coach next morning for the day's sightseeing program, both the Hansons took a good look at Celia. Mrs. Hanson's mouth became even more discontented-looking, and she gave her Edward a nudge. He said something reassuring in a low voice, but she shook her head in violent disagreement and treated Celia to a very theatrical smile. She's recognized me, Celia thought, and he's trying to persuade her that she hasn't. Do I put them out of their misery and say: Yes it's me, what are you doing here? Or don't I?

Nigel Monk was beckoning her into a vacant seat next to him, and Major Gatling looked up expectantly from his place near the back. She ignored both of them and sat down next to the Armstrongs' tousle-haired daughter, who threw her an unwelcoming glance and turned to stare out of the window. The coach started off, and Professor Winkworth seized the microphone.

"Good morning everyone, I hope you slept well. Let me just tell you today's program. This morning we go to Settignano to visit I Tatti, the home of the late Bernard Berenson, which is now the Center for Italian Renaissance Studies of Harvard University. The garden there is strictly private, but an exception is being made for us as a 'special interest group', and we are indeed privileged to see it. We shall lunch at a *trattoria* in Settignano which our friend Paolo here has cleverly found for us, and after that we are to be lucky enough to see two more private gardens which are never open to the public, belonging to Sir Harold Acton and the Marchesa Tibaldi. Now, if anyone has any questions, I will try to answer them."

"I have one," said Mr. Price, wagging his self-important little beard. "Why must we have lunch in Settignano? If we went into the centre of Florence we could get a snack somewhere and have a quick look at the Uffizi or the Bargello before we go on to these other villas."

Assuming a charming smile of apology, Paolo squashed this flat. "The centre of Florence is not civilized, it is a barbarity of petrol smells and noise and half-naked tourists. To drive in and out again in the midday rush would be a madness; moreover at twelve o'clock they are shutting the Bargello and Uffizi galleries and all the other touristic things, to go there would be a nonsense."

The Prices grumbled about this to the people behind them through the hole between their headrests, and Celia decided to see if she could make the Armstrong daughter stop sulking. "Hullo," she said. "I'm Celia, what's your name?"

The girl brushed some of the mousy hair aside, revealing rather pretty features. "I'm Jane, Jane Armstrong. I suppose gardens turn you on."

"Some do, some give me the creeps. I'm not sure I shall go for this lot. How about you?"

"In my present mood I'd cheerfully vandalize the Garden of Eden," Jane replied.

"That seems a bit drastic. Why are you on this tour then?"

"Guess."

"Are you being rescued from the clutches of an unsuitable boyfriend?"

"No, but you're not far out. Try again."

"Is it your politics that are unsuitable?"

"Bang on, that was clever of you."

"There's something wrong with anyone your age who takes their politics ready-made from their parents. Whose political clutches are you supposed to be in?"

"The point is, I go on anti-nuclear marches. So they have dire visions of what I might get up to if they left me in charge of the house while they were away. You know, verminous anarchists lolling in the drawing-room and women's libbers having it off with each other in all the beds. Why d'you think you won't like these gardens?"

"It's flowers that turn me on, and there won't be many interesting ones. Mostly huge evergreen hedges and fountains with statues attached, I gather. And—oh dear, look at that."

There was a nursery garden beside the motorway. It contained row upon row of young *Magnolia grandiflora* trained into a conical shape, like toy Christmas trees. She had seen full-grown specimens of the same horrid trick in gardens near the hotel. "There, Jane. You see what I mean. The Italians make very grand gardens, but they have no sense of cruelty to vegetation. Fancy doing that to a magnificent forest tree."

They chatted amicably till the coach halted in the main street of Settignano.

"Why are we stopping here?" asked the Professor.

"*Scusi, Signor Professore*," said Paolo. "I am not knowing well Settignano. We go to I Tatti, I think, Berenson villa. Which way must we go from here?"

The Professor peered out vaguely through the windscreen. "Don't ask me, my dear fellow."

"But you have been there before, I think."

"Yes, three months ago when I went to make the arrangements, but I was in a taxi and took no notice. Could the driver ask someone?"

Having got directions, the driver deposited his coachload at the entrance to I Tatti. Farthingale Tours trooped through the library block which had been added to the notorious old connoisseur's villa by the Centre for Renaissance Studies, and out into the garden beyond. Its main feature combined everything Celia disliked about formal Italian gardens. A terraced slope, flowerless and covered with shrubs trimmed into geometrical shapes, led down to a pair of marble-lined pools of the sort which have to be referred to in a historical garden context as tanks. But there were charming corners elsewhere, banks of snow-white azaleas, roses high on a wall, and a lemon garden presided over by a bust of Bernard Berenson.

"He was a naughty old gentleman, I think," said Paolo, coming up to Celia as she studied it. "He collected much money from dealers for telling Americans that pictures were genuine when they were not."

This seemed a curious piece of knowledge for a travel agency courier to possess. "What d'you do when you're not herding tourists about?" Celia asked.

"I work for a firm, very dull. This is first time I am courier, a girl I know was to do it, but she breaked her leg skiing and she said, Why don't I take her place? And I said, Yes, why not? It's fun. Only now I think perhaps it's not fun, the charming Professor is not practical and does not know where to go."

Near a turn in a path, Lady Carstairs was burying her fluffy white head in a flowering shrub in a terracotta vase. "Come, Mrs. Hanson," she said. "Feast your eyes and your nose on this sweet-smelling reminder of home."

"Oh. Yes. Charming," said Mrs. Hanson without enthusiasm.

Several people had gathered round to look at the plant. An unspoken question hung in the air until the deplorable George voiced it. "Know what it is, do yer?"

"How silly," said Mrs. Hanson. "The name's on the tip of my tongue."

"*Brunfelsia calycina*," Lady Carstairs announced. "Widely known among your fellow-countrymen as 'Yesterday, Today, Tomorrow' because it marks the melancholy passage of time. The flowers take three days to change from violet to mauve, then white, after which they die amid the intoxication of their successors' perfume."

Celia came to Mrs. Hanson's defense by pointing out that *Brunfelsia calycina* was not a South African native, but came from Brazil. Had the Carstairs couple penetrated Mrs. Hanson's false pretenses, and were they deliberately drawing public attention to her ignorance? If so, why?

Lunch-time came, but owing to the Professor's lax attitude to the timetable, Farthingale Tours would have fasted through it if Paolo had not taken the situation in hand. He collected the party from all over the garden, and got it into the coach and back to Settignano for lunch.

Nigel Monk, who was Celia's neighbour at table, turned to her with what was meant to be a fascinating smile. "Tell me about yourself," he commanded.

Celia was determined to do no such thing. Claiming to be Miss Grant from Devon had been a disastrous mistake. Inventing a morass of lies about her life there would only make matters worse. "I'm not at all an interesting person," she replied. "I'd much rather hear about you."

He twinkled at her through the rimless glasses. "No. You decide to remain a woman of mystery, so I shall wrap myself in mystery too."

When Farthingale Tours boarded the coach again after lunch, there was a major crisis. Lady Carstairs' camera was missing. Knowing that the coach would be locked while the driver had his lunch, she had left it on her seat instead of taking it into the restaurant. After an embarrassed general search, it was found in the parcel rack above Mrs. Hanson's seat, under her cardigan.

Lady Carstairs let a startled exclamation fall from her painted lips and directed an accusing stare at Mrs. Hanson. The hubbub of search had subsided, and everyone was wondering silently what on earth had prompted her to pinch someone else's camera and hide it under her cardigan. Mrs. Hanson's lips moved in some inaudible reply to this unspoken question, and she turned with tears in her eyes to stare out of the window. "Extraordinary," Nigel Monk murmured as he passed Celia's seat. "Kleptomania coupled with a guilty desire to be found out. The woman must be schizoid."

Celia had to agree that if Mrs. Hanson was a kleptomaniac she was a very stupid one. The camera was almost certain to be found as soon as it was missed.

The first stop of the afternoon was at Sir Harold Acton's Villa la Petraia, which stood at the end of another long cypress avenue. Before letting Farthingale Tours wander round it, the Professor delivered a brief lecture.

"Despite appearances, this is not a historic Italian garden," he began. "It was created in the present century, and is a romantic Englishman's idea of what an Italian Renaissance garden should be like."*

It was certainly a romantic garden. High evergreen hedges formed long grass alleys with statues at the end of them, giving an effect of nostalgic melancholy. As the party spread out into it, Celia saw the Hansons disappear into one of the smaller enclosures opening off the main axis. Since the episode in the coach with the camera, they had been muttering angrily to each other at intervals, as if they disagreed about it, and Celia suspected that they had gone in there to have their disagreement out in private. Would they realize, though, that a grass enclosure surrounded by high hedges was not necessarily soundproof? Perhaps not, anyway it was worth trying. She crept into the next of these open-air rooms, which was dominated by a bust of a cross-looking Roman emperor, and prepared to eavesdrop.

But the Hansons were keeping their voices low, and she could only deduce from their tones that Mrs. Hanson was angry with her Edward for some reason, and was being made even angrier by the feebleness of his attempts to defend himself. Presently she became too enraged to keep her voice down. "I know she said Devon, but there's no pass law that says people from Devon are barred from setting foot in Sussex. I'm dead sure it's her."

Edward's reply was inaudible, and she stormed on. "She hasn't rumbled us yet, but any moment she will. What happens then? Calamity. You got me into this, you get me out."

Edward shushed her, then went on speaking in a low murmur. It sounded as if he was protesting that, on the

---

*"It was in poetry, in imagination that the great Renaissance garden makers reigned supreme, and inspiration is a breath of the muses which may not be brought within the rules of art. Their first thought was for the aesthetic impression on the individual . . . for chords struck upon those vague, nebulous spectral feelings which are ever trembling upon the threshold of consciousness." (Sir George Sitwell, *An Essay on the Making of Gardens*. London 1909)

contrary, whatever fix they were in was her fault, not his. Presently she burst out again. "How dare they pull that filthy trick with the camera? Setting me up as a half-mad thief in front of a whole busload of people. I won't stand for it, I want out."

Suddenly Edward lost his temper too. "You can't. If you do they'll give you more of the same, only worse. You've got to keep our bargain, do what they want us to do."

"No way. That woman could blow the whole thing wide open and land us all in jail."

"She hasn't recognized us yet. You're not even sure it's her."

"Yes I am, and I mean what I say. I shall tell Professor Winkworth there's illness in the family and we have to go home."

A noisy intrusion of Farthingaleites wielding cameras prevented Celia from hearing more, but she had heard quite enough. Damn, she thought. They aren't fantasizing. They're strapped for money, and they've let themselves be tempted into crime. Heaven knows what sort of crime, but anyway, bang go my hopes of a quiet mystery-free holiday. And the worst of it is that I'll be waiting from moment to moment for the mystery to happen.

Correction, that was not quite true. Part of the mystery had happened already. The people Mrs. Hanson called "they" had put someone else's camera under her cardigan to warn her of the treatment she could expect if she tried to back out of her bargain. And from this an alarming conclusion followed. "They" were not arch-criminals masterminding the Hansons from London or Rome. They were travelling with Farthingale Tours on the coach.

As before, Professor Winkworth made no attempt to gather his flock together when it was time to move on. In the end Paolo had to round everyone up, but by then Farthingale Tours was going to be sensationally late for its next appointment at the Marchesa Tibaldi's.

"I hope the dear Professor knows where is this next

place," Paolo muttered, "because I am not knowing at all."

His hopes were ill-founded. Betrayed by the Professor's faulty sense of direction, the coach wandered aimlessly in the maze of lanes round Soffiano till the driver, tiring of this, made enquiries, backtracked several kilometres, and deposited his charges at the lower end of a lane which he said was too narrow for his coach. The party toiled uphill on foot to the sixteenth century villa whose garden they were to view. But as they walked in through the great gates and up to the house, its front door was opened by a white-coated manservant. The Marchesa Tibaldi, an imposing elderly lady, appeared in the doorway to shake hands with everyone and invite them into the house, whereupon it became embarrassingly clear that Farthingale Tours had arrived hot, unsuitably dressed and very late, for an elaborate tea-party in their honour.

The prospect of tea triggered off an immediate revolt by the Prices, who asked if they might use the telephone to summon a taxi. They had no intention of wasting their time over such foppery when they could be down in Florence admiring the Baptistry doors and the Duomo.

"Then you will come back here later to rejoin the party?" asked the Professor.

"We thought you could pick us up outside the Duomo on your way back to the hotel."

"We do not go back through the middle of Florence," said Paolo. "You must take train to Montecatini and taxi to the hotel."

As the Prices went off crossly to telephone, Nigel Monk attached himself once more to Celia. "I do enjoy those two," he murmured. "They're not really culture vultures. More like culture mice, don't you think?"

An army of servants had begun pouring tea from silver teapots and handing round tiny sandwiches and cakes.

"How very kind of the Marchesa," said Professor Wink-worth, munching cake. "I had no reason to expect anything like this."

The Marchesa's garden was an anticlimax after her tea, since many of its formal features had been destroyed during the nineteenth-century vogue for naturalistic landscape gardening in the English style. Even the Professor was not tempted to linger, and the party returned more or less punctually for dinner at the hotel. Celia changed, and took her place at one of the tables reserved for the Farthingale Tours party. Major Gatling was hot on her heels, and slipped into the place next to her. Nigel Monk, beaten to it in a photo finish, sat down opposite and treated her to a jolly, conspiratorial wink.

At the end of the table, the Professor had the Armstrongs on one side of him and the shy, silent young Enderby-Scotts on the other. The remaining places were filled by the Hansons and by Lady Carstairs and George, who chalked up another black mark by smoking during the first course, and stubbing out his cigarette in his half-eaten spaghetti when Mrs. Armstrong complained.

The Professor launched out into a learned discourse about the influence of classical antiquity on Renaissance garden design, but was called to the telephone in the middle of it. He returned looking alarmed. "The call was from the Marchesa," he reported. "Something very unfortunate has happened. A theft."

Everyone exclaimed in dismay, and Mrs. Armstrong asked what had been stolen.

"A silver cream ewer dating from the seventeenth century, rather valuable. It was found to be missing when the tea was cleared away. The Marchesa says her servants have been with her for years and are completely trustworthy. Apart from members of her family, no one was present but ourselves. The implication is that one of us must have taken it."

"Oh no!" cried Mrs. Hanson loudly. "It's disgraceful, how dare they?"

❦ TWO ❦

In the embarrassed silence which followed, Mrs. Armstrong became very much the colonel's lady with a duty to give a lead in an emergency. "Now, Professor. This sort of thing's very nasty, but it's no use beating about the bush, is it? Everyone's room must be searched. I'll organize it for you, shall I?"

"It's very kind of you to offer," said the Professor. "But as I am supposed to be in charge of this expedition, I feel I should do whatever proves necessary myself."

Mrs. Armstrong looked round the dinner-table, inviting everyone to share her doubts about his competence. "Of course, but the searching has to be done by someone who's not a suspect. We could get the manager of the hotel to do it for us. How big is this ewer thing?"

"I'm afraid I forgot to ask. Quite small, I imagine. One doesn't need enormous jugs for cream."

"Then it may be small enough to fit into a woman's handbag or a man's pocket. We must have the people searched as well as their rooms."

Mrs. Hanson dived under the table for her handbag and started an alarmed scrambling in it. Having found no stolen

31

silver among its contents, she pretended that all she wanted from it was a handkerchief and calmed down.

The Prices came into the restaurant, very late for dinner but hotfoot from Florence. They were in an ecstasy of cultural superiority, having mingled with Italians in a bus in addition to admiring the Baptistry doors and the Duomo. Mrs. Armstrong intercepted them on their way to a table, and brought them down to earth with the shocking news about the Marchesa's cream jug.

"This is no concern of ours," said Mr. Price. "We were not present at that ridiculous bun-fight, and I forbid you to have our room searched. If you do, I shall make a formal complaint to the tour operator."

The Prices moved on to sit at another table, leaving regrets behind them. If anyone was to be convicted of theft, they would have been a popular choice.

"What've they got up in their bedroom then?" George inquired. "A mass of leather sex aids and dirty postcards, I bet."

"Enormous hoards of fibrous health foods," murmured Nigel Monk.

"Why should they be hiding anything?" Jane Armstrong protested. "How d'you know they aren't just asserting their human rights?"

Her mother gave Jane a withering look, then started bullying the Professor again with proposals for organizing the search.

"I'll do anything," interrupted Mrs. Hanson in her Lady Macbeth voice. "Whatever's wanted, I'm absolutely willing." Her husband nodded approval, to convey that she had said the right thing. Everyone else looked at her in surprise. She had spoken as if making a public announcement to the whole table.

"Everyone should be searched as they leave the dining-room, Professor," urged Mrs. Armstrong. "If you let them go to their rooms, they'd be able to hide the thing somewhere on the way."

The Professor, deep in unhappy thought, took no notice, but Mrs. Hanson repeated her announcement. "I'll co-operate, I'm absolutely willing to co-operate."

Suddenly Celia grasped what all this was about. Mrs. Hanson was addressing a hidden message to "them": Please don't put the silver jug in our room and brand me as a kleptomaniac, I've changed my mind, I won't back out, I'll do what you want.

The conclusion which followed from this insight was rather alarming. Mrs. Hanson's broadcast message only made sense if "they" were sitting at table with her to receive it.

Who? She looked round at her fellow-diners. The young, shy-seeming Enderby-Scotts. Lady Carstairs with her painted face and pussycat airs. Her deplorable George, who had just said "Pardon me" to excuse a belch, and was lighting yet another cigarette. Major Gatling, the bright-eyed, dapper little soldier: Nigel Monk, with his gingery beard and his air of detached amusement. Professor Wink-worth, who must surely be ruled out on grounds of im-probability. Finally, the Armstrong family. Mrs. Armstrong was a determined woman, who seemed to have her husband well under her thumb. If she had made up her mind to rob a bank, she would have organized a team of regimental wives to do it as firmly as she had organized them into providing the tea at cricket matches. But would she have lumbered herself with a rebellious teenage daughter if she was planning to mastermind a crime?

She was still trying to organize Professor Winkworth. "Well, Professor, what do you intend to do?"

The Professor rose from the table. "I shall ask everyone to go straight to the lounge after dinner, for an important announcement."

"Giving them time to hide the thing somewhere on the way?" she protested.

The Professor treated her to a charming smile. "I think

33

it will be best if I am left to deal with this matter in my own way."

"Quite right, Winkworth," said Colonel Armstrong. "Pipe down, Dolly. Let the man in charge get on with the job."

While the Professor went round delivering his summons at the other Farthingale Tours tables, the company he left behind was plunged in gloom. Mrs. Armstrong made herself responsible for the maintenance of civilized decencies amid disaster, and started a dinner-table conversation which she kept going by sheer will-power. When her efforts ground to a halt, her husband discovered that he and Major Gatling had military acquaintances in common, and the whole table listened in silence while they decided that neither of them had seen Buffles Watson lately, and that Lofty Perkins had always been a bit of a card. Mrs. Hanson was eating nothing, and stared at her plate as if at her breakfast in the condemned cell. When it was removed and replaced by a large portion of *crème caramel*, she stared at it as if it might bite her, and ignored whispered exhortations by her husband to try to behave normally.

After dinner Farthingale Tours assembled obediently in the lounge to hear the Professor's announcement. He told them about the theft and went on to explain what he proposed to do about it. "I do not intend to organize an immediate search of all the rooms and everyone's personal possessions—"

"Why not?" asked Mrs. Armstrong.

"Because if the ewer was taken by a professional thief, he or she will have expected a search to take place, and will have made sure the stolen object is where we won't find it. All the circumstances suggest that it was taken by one of us in a fit of mental aberration, the sort of thing that can happen to perfectly respectable and upright people when, for instance, they are under stress for some reason. I'm sure you all know what I'm talking about. I therefore propose to give the person concerned an opportunity to

34

correct his or her error without unpleasant consequences. I ask him or her to place the ewer in a prominent position in one of the corridors or public rooms during the night. No watch will be kept, and no attempt will be made to identify the culprit. I shall ask the manager to have a search made at six tomorrow morning. If the ewer is still missing then, I shall cancel tomorrow's excursion and put the matter in the hands of the police.''

A buzz of anxious conversation followed.

"Well we all know who done it," said George Johnson, glancing across the room towards the Hansons. "Stands to reason, after what happened to Ma's camera."

Jane Armstrong had overheard this, and planted herself in front of George. "That was horrible of you. It was slander, you've got no evidence."

Celia rallied to Jane's support. "I think we should be very careful what we say about Mrs. Hanson. Appearances can be very deceptive."

An unmentionable subject had been opened up to general debate by interested parties. Mr. Price remarked that no good could be expected of white South Africans. Why not, demanded the dainty editress of a flower-arranging magazine. Why was it more virtuous for blacks to be murdering and burning and spreading revolution than it was for whites to be standing up to defend civilization against the tide of barbarism? The Prices took issue with this, but she shouted them down. The elegant bachelor from Norfolk tried to say that a lot of white South Africans were very liberal, but was shouted down both by the Prices, who said that rich white South Africans were by definition not liberal, and by the flower-arranging lady, who said that any who were were probably crypto-communists. Celia said nothing. She was too busy with her thoughts.

She was intercepted on her way up to her room by Jane Armstrong. "Thanks for supporting me, Celia. He had no business to talk like that about Mrs. Hanson, had he?"

"No. You were quite right to say what you did."

"It was weird, wasn't it, the way Mrs. Hanson said she'd do anything people wanted. I mean, out loud like that as if she was anxious for everyone to hear. It was almost as if she was appealing for help, sort of. I wish I knew why."

Celia did know, and was strongly tempted to tell Jane the whole story. But was it fair to burden anyone so young with what she knew? Moreover, was it wise? Jane had a very acute sense of justice, and might insist on taking damagingly hotheaded action. Celia resisted the temptation and withdrew to her room to think.

Was she to prowl the corridors all night and try to identify the jug's purloiner? It would be risky, and perhaps unwise. The Professor had promised that no watch would be kept for the culprit. If "they" discovered that someone was patrolling the corridors, they would probably decide not to give the jug back, so that suspicion went on pointing at the unfortunate Mrs. Hanson.

Next morning at breakfast, Farthingale Tours was divided between those who avoided discussing the theft and those who could talk of nothing else. The Hansons were conspicuous by their absence, and the Professor too had not appeared. Mrs. Armstrong went round the tables urging everyone to be very kind to him, because he was "not up to dealing with this sort of thing". When he did appear, he looked haggard, as if after a sleepless night, and he had cut himself shaving. But he was triumphant. The precious ewer had been found on a table in the lounge when the hotel was searched in the early morning, and he had brought it in to show them. It was a beautiful thing, delicately ornamented with a flower pattern.

"I've telephoned the news to the Marchesa," he said, "and as her property's been recovered she's quite happy for the matter not to be taken any further."

"But that leaves us all under an intolerable weight of suspicion," Mrs. Armstrong protested.

"Not really, we know what happened," said the lugubrious woman in black. "It was taken by that vulgar, rich

South African woman. And her husband got it off her and put it in the lounge during the night."

Jane looked mutinous, but her parents were glaring at her forbiddingly and she said nothing. Celia was tempted to explain that Mrs. Hanson was neither rich nor South African in any relevant sense of the word. But she decided that it would involve more complications than she could face so soon after breakfast.

When the time came to leave for the day's expedition the Hansons, looking relieved, were among the last to board the coach. They uttered a series of defiant "good mornings" as they moved down the aisle to their seats, but received only silence or embarrassed murmurs in reply. "How can they be so beastly?" Jane Armstrong murmured to Celia. "I wish I could think of a way to make it up to her."

Professor Winkworth went off separately in a taxi to make his peace with the Marchesa, with the ewer carefully wrapped in tissue paper. He rejoined the main party at its first sightseeing point of the day, the Villa Gamberaia at Settignano. The long cypress avenue leading to it was lined with hedges of a pretty little pink shrub rose in full bloom, and everyone wondered what it was. The Prices advanced on a gardener with their phrasebook at the ready, extracted from him the word "*bossolo*", and were soon telling anyone who would listen that this was the name of the rose.

"It would be cruel to disillusion them," murmured Professor Winkworth, "but '*bossolo*' is the Italian for box. He thought they were asking about the little hedges round the beds."

"It's a China, isn't it?" said Mrs. Enderby-Scott shyly. "I think it's called Old Blush.''*

Questioned by Celia, she proved to be a customer of a famous firm which grew old-fashioned roses, and her knowl-

---

*This rose was among the first of the Chinas to arrive in Europe around the end of the eighteenth century. Its Italian name is "Lengalesia" and it is still much used as a hedging rose in Tuscan gardens. The descendants of these China roses are responsible for the perpetual-flowering strain in modern hybrid teas and floribundas.

edge of its catalogue was very detailed. This struck Celia as odd, the Enderby-Scotts claimed to live in London and have no garden. She tried to discover more, but the husband was standing guard, and soon found a means of putting an end to the conversation without giving offense. There was something chilly about them both, Celia decided, which a detailed knowledge of the old roses did not dispel.

Behind the villa, an elaborate parterre of formal flower-beds and marble tanks was enclosed by tall evergreen hedges. But the beds had been planted out delightfully and were full of color. Celia was enjoying them quietly when she was ambushed half-way down the central path by Nigel Monk.

"Celia!" he said, putting an arm round her shoulders. "You are avoiding me. Why?"

She shook off his arm. "I wasn't aware that I was."

"You wouldn't sit next to me in the coach. It was the same last night at dinner."

She cursed the morbid vanity of men. "I have nothing against you, but a woman travelling alone doesn't want to become the exclusive property of an unattached male in the same party."

"I don't see why not, if they hit it off together."

"I wasn't aware that we had," she said coldly and turned to go. But he detained her with a warm hand on her bare arm. "One moment, what have we here?"

A smartly dressed woman had come out of the villa with two Pekinese dogs and taken them to drink out of one of the marble tanks.

"She must be the owner," Nigel murmured. "Do something for me, Celia."

"It depends. What?"

"Suggest to the Prices that they should ask her about the '*bossolo*' rose."

"Certainly not, you must make your own mischief."

"No fear. Getting other people to is much more fun."

"Your sense of fun is very perverted," she said, and

retreated down a long green bowling alley into a secret garden at the end, with a fountain presided over by a nude male effigy with goatish horns and a trident. As she wondered whether it represented Neptune or Pan, she was attacked from behind by Major Gatling, who had been an interested witness to her encounter with Nigel Monk.

"Quite right to give that feller the push," said the dapper little soldier. "He wouldn't do you a bit of good. Too big and clumsy. Gay too, I shouldn't wonder."

Two of them in one morning was more than Celia could bear. "Mr. Monk's sexual orientation is no concern of yours or mine."

Unabashed, Major Gatling fixed her with eyes like urgent blue poached-eggs. "You should try me, why don't you? I may be small but I'm hot stuff."

"Thank you, but I'm not interested in casual holiday fornication," said Celia.

"Sorry if I spoke out of turn." He walked away with a self-satisfied smile, as if under the impression that he had paid her a compliment.

Celia was suddenly suspicious. The Major had been at the dinner-table when Mrs. Hanson made her appeal to "them", saying she would "do anything" rather than be branded as a kleptomaniac who had stolen a valuable piece of silver. Perhaps he had not been overcome by her charms. Perhaps he had calculated coldly that getting her into bed would be the easiest way of finding out whether she was the person Mrs. Hanson thought she was.

Nigel Monk had been at the dinner-table too. His approach had been slightly less crude, but the same suspicion applied to him. It could even apply to both of them. Mrs. Hanson's remarks suggested more than one person, but "they" did not have to be travelling together openly as a couple.

At the end of a long grass alley, Mrs. Hanson was admiring a small flowering tree.

"Oh, look!" she cried. "A white laburnum."

A well-bred silence was Farthingale Tours' instinctive response to this horticultural solecism. It would have been crude to point out to her that the tree in question was not a laburnum, but a white wistaria grown as a standard, and nobody did. Instead, cameras were raised to photograph it, and Mrs. Hanson moved out of range.

"No, do please stay where you are," called the bachelor from Norfolk from behind his view-finder. "One needs a figure to give the scale."

Mrs. Hanson ignored this and walked away. "Ethel hates having her picture taken," Mr. Hanson explained to the company at large.

Could Mrs. Hanson's name really be Ethel? Surely not. Anything so old-fashioned and odd would have stuck in Celia's mind. And no wonder she refused to be photographed, it was a wise precaution if she was masquerading as someone else. Celia wished she had brought her own camera, to take snaps of the Hansons on the sly. But she never did when on holiday, preferring memories of things she had looked at carefully to a clutch of photographs stuffed away in drawers.

The Gamberaia garden, though privately owned, was open to the public. There were some non-Farthingale visitors about, among them two slim, elegant black men who stood on the edge of the group waiting for the photography to be over before passing in front of the cameras. The bachelor from Norfolk, still in search of a figure to give the scale, decided that black faces and white wistaria racemes added up to something very rococo and tried to press them into service as models. They declined in modest embarrassment, and Celia wondered why. A primitive belief that photography stole away one's life force? Surely not, these were not naked savages. Why then?

Had she seen them before? She had noticed two black men sitting on a wall near the restaurant in Settignano where the party had lunched the previous day, and had wondered who they were and where they were from. Were these the same two? Probably not, it must be a coincidence.

As usual everyone was ready to leave the Villa Gamberaia long before Professor Winkworth gave the signal to move off. They waited on a terrace with fantastic stone animals along its balustrade, overlooking a superb view. Celia found herself next to the Prices, who began asking her about various people who they were certain she must know in Lynton. Disclaiming acquaintance with any of them, she alleged that the Lynton cottage was really a holiday home.

"Yet you gave the tour operator that address," said Mr. Price on an exaggerated note of surprise. "Do tell us where you really live."

Anywhere but Sussex, Celia thought, acutely aware that the Hansons were listening avidly. "I . . . have a flat in London," she managed.

Evadne Price studied her with beady venom. "You're not wearing your wedding-ring."

"But you were wearing it when you arrived at Pisa airport," added her husband.

She was covered with shame. I am in the Farthingale Tours doghouse now, she told herself, along with Mrs. Hanson the kleptomaniac and the subversive Prices and the terrible Lady Carstairs with her rent boy. I am suspected of having removed my wedding-ring in the hope of a holiday love-affair, and nobody except those two lust-ridden men will want to have anything to do with me.

By the time Paolo initiated a move down into Florence for lunch, she had recovered enough presence of mind to wonder about the motives for the Prices' attack. Were they part of the Hanson conspiracy, and had they been told to undermine her credibility before she denounced the Hansons as impostors? Probably not, she was getting conspiracies on the brain. The Prices had probably rubbished her out of motiveless natural malice.

The party lunched in a *trattoria* in down-town Florence. The Prices excused themselves again and hived off to steep themselves in Florentine culture. The rest of Farthingale Tours went on to the Iris Garden, on the flank of the hill below the Piazza Michelangelo. This visit to the Mecca of the iris world was the high point of Celia's visit to Italy, and she tried to shut everything else out of her mind and learn as much as she could.

The whole hillside was covered with a mass of bearded iris in full bloom, and the scent was heady. The patch being judged consisted of rhizomes sent in by their growers the previous year, and now in flower for the first time. Elsewhere on the slope, entries from earlier years had been kept in cultivation for comparison and reference. An English-speaking iris specialist was giving the group a guided lecture tour and Celia tried to clarify her mind about the finer points of color, scent and habit which separated what the English-speaking expert called "rubbish" from the short list of entries from serious competitors.*

But half her mind was busy with the fact that the two camera-shy black men she had noticed at the Villa Gamberaia were trailing Farthingale Tours round the garden. She kept reminding herself that they had as much right as anyone else to be there, and that if they were English speakers it was understandable for them to hover on the fringes of a party that was being lectured to in English. Coincidence? Possibly. But it left her uneasy.

I must control myself and not have persecution mania, she told herself. Perhaps the Hansons are who they say they are, and just happen to bear a resemblance to a pair of broken-down actors with a Down's syndrome child whom I saw once for an hour or two last year. Perhaps I misunderstood what I managed to overhear of their conversation in Sir Harold Acton's garden. She had woken twice in the

---

*To qualify in Florence, an iris must have seven blooms, three on the terminal spike and two each on well-displayed side branches. In the 1986 competition, so many of the entries lacked this essential that the supply of stakes marked "E" for "eliminated" ran out. They had to be pulled up and put in beside different entries, with "E" standing for "eligible" instead.

small hours filled with self-doubt, and it came flooding back now. It was idiotic to get oneself into a high old state about two black men who just happened to be following the same tourist-round as her group.

The coach was waiting for them on the Piazza Michelangelo. At an ice-cream stall near it, a woman was handing an ice-cream to a pasty-faced child in dark glasses, perhaps eight or ten years old, with distorted features and a shambling gait. Recognizing the characteristic signs of Down's syndrome, Celia stole a look at Ethel Hanson. She had seen it too, and was gazing intently at the child as it licked messily at its ice-cream. Her husband noticed Celia watching her and pulled at her arm. Still looking back at the child, she climbed into the coach.

Celia was reassured. She was not mistaken about the Hansons. But she was also alarmed. After what had just happened, the Hansons must know that she had recognized them.

During the ride back to the hotel, Jane Armstrong said: "Would you mind awfully giving me some money? I'd say 'lend' but it's no use pretending I'd ever be able to pay it back."

"It depends. How much, and what for?"

"Enough to buy a bunch of flowers for Mrs. Hanson. They've been horrible to her all day, not talking to her and looking down their noses. It's no use asking my parents, they wouldn't approve."

Celia herself was unsure. "You don't think Mrs. Hanson would be embarrassed?"

"Oh, I shan't tell her why, I shall just push them at her."

It was a generous impulse. Perhaps it deserved support. "I think I could manage enough for that," said Celia, and handed over what she thought was a suitable sum.

"Thanks a lot. I'll go and buy them as soon as the coach gets back. There must be a flower shop somewhere down in the town."

Back in her hotel room, Celia applied herself to the telephone. Not knowing the Hansons' real name irked her, and it was worth the expense of a call to England to discover it. Her uncle Hugo had a tidy habit of keeping theatre programs, so she tried him first. There was no reply, and she remembered that he was visiting friends in Madeira. Then she tried the Claytons, in the hope that they would remember the name of their house guests with the Down's syndrome son. But they seemed to be out, so she bathed and changed, then settled down in the lounge behind the unaccustomed luxury of a Campari-soda. But it soon occurred to her that she owed various people postcards. After a long wait in the crowd round the desk, she managed to buy some and settled down to write them, fortified by sips of the Campari-soda.

It was not a drink she was used to. Did it always taste so strong? Perhaps it was an illusion, and she persevered. But by the time she wrote the address of the third postcard, she was beginning to feel very peculiar.

A shadow fell across the table and she looked up. A grimfaced committee of enquiry confronted her, consisting of Colonel and Mrs. Armstrong.

"Ah Miss Grant, I wonder if you can help us," the Colonel began.

"Jane's nowhere in the hotel," Mrs. Armstrong added accusingly. "When last seen, she was sitting beside you in the coach."

"Yes. When we got out, she went down into the town to buy some flowers."

"But that was over an hour ago, and she's not back."

"Flowers?" the Colonel echoed in a voice squeaky with surprise. "What did she want with flowers?"

"She wanted to give some to Mrs. Hanson, because she thought everyone had treated her rather unkindly."

"But I don't understand," said Mrs. Armstrong. "Jane hasn't any Italian money to buy flowers with."

"No. I gave her some," said Celia.

"You gave our daughter money?" asked Mrs. Armstrong. "How extraordinary. Why?"

Disconcerted, Celia reached automatically for her suspect drink and took a long swig. "It seemed a reasonable request. I agree with her that Mrs. Hanson's been rather unfairly treated."

Mrs. Armstrong turned to her husband. "You see, Teddy? Now she'll spend half the night in some filthy discotheque."

"All I gave her was the price of a bunch of carnations," Celia managed, despite her increased giddiness. "I doubt if it would get her into one."

Mrs. Armstrong greeted this with well-bred impatience. "I'm sure you didn't mean to behave irresponsibly, but thanks to you she's on the loose in a strange town where she doesn't know the language, getting up to goodness knows what."

Emboldened by drink, Celia let everything hang out. "Why shouldn't Jane go where she can see a few people her own age? If anyone's irresponsible you are, dragging a girl like that on an older-generation tour of a lot of mouldy old gardens which bore her out of her mind. No wonder she slips away when she can if you never trust her with enough money to buy even a few flowers when she wants to."

She rose, staggered, and fell back into her chair. Decidedly, there was something wrong with the Campari.

"You're blind drunk," said Mrs. Armstrong, as Celia rose again and swayed on her feet.

True, thought Celia. I am very drunk. Moreover, I must somehow make it to the ladies' before I vomit.

"Excuse me," she managed, and staggered away in what she hoped was the right direction.

"Well, really!" said Mrs. Armstrong, raising her eyebrows as she watched her go.

After spending a miserable quarter of an hour in the lavatory, Celia decided she could not face dinner and withdrew to her room, where she took stock. Her drink had been doctored. When? While she was at the desk buying postcards. Who by? Anyone, she had been away for at least ten minutes, with her drink sitting unguarded on a low table in the lounge. How? Order oneself a double gin or whisky and pour it into the Campari, reckoning rightly that an Englishwoman, unaccustomed to the strong, bitter taste, would fail to notice the difference. Why? Because the Hansons knew she had recognized them, they had seen her take note of Ethel's interest in the Down's syndrome child with the ice-cream. Dear me, she thought. I have taken off my wedding-ring to ensnare a man for myself; been caught out pretending to live in Devon when I don't; funded subversive activities by Jane Armstrong and been rude to her parents; and now to top everything I have been drunk and disorderly in a public place. So if I announce to the world that the Hansons are impostors whose real name I don't know, no one will believe me.

Presently she began to feel well enough to ring the Claytons again, but they were still out. As she put the phone down there was a knock at the door. "Who's there?"

"Clean towels," said an Italian-sounding male voice.

She sat up in a daze. Her towels had been changed that morning. Whoever heard of a male chambermaid? And why did he knock instead of using his pass key? During the dinner hour he would expect the room to be empty.

"Don't bother, you can change them in the morning," she called.

Ten minutes had passed, and she was beginning to feel better, when there was another knock on the door. "Miss Grant? It's Mrs. Hanson. I'm told you've been taken ill, we're worried about you. May I come in?"

"Thank you, but I'm perfectly all right. Really."

There were murmurings out in the passage. Someone else was out there, prompting her.

"I've got my first-aid box here," she said, sounding frightened. "I'm sure there's something in it that would help. Do let me in."

You and who else? Celia thought. To do what? Administer some lethal dose from the first-aid box? No, that would show up at the post mortem. Something more subtle. "Drunken Englishwoman's fatal fall from hotel balcony", how about that?

"Will you please go away," she said crossly, "I'm perfectly all right."

So she was, as long as she stayed locked in her bedroom. But "they" knew she was a danger to them, and for the rest of the tour they would be a danger to her.

Who were "they"? Once again, she ran over her list of suspects. The Professor was in the clear. So were the Armstrongs, if only because Mrs. Armstrong would not have bullied the Professor to search for the jug at once if they were the addressees of Mrs. Hanson's plea for mercy. Nigel Monk and the Major were likely starters, and so were the mysteriously cold and unsociable Enderby-Scotts. Rent boys were by definition part of the criminal underworld, and the Carstairs carry-on was so odd that it could easily be a front for something. Tomorrow, one of these people would try to push her under a car or over a precipice. What could she do about that?

After a lot of thought she hit on a plan which might work. But she would need an accomplice. It would have to be Jane Armstrong, there was no one else. Had Jane really gone out on the tiles? She rang her bedroom to see, and found her in.

"Hullo, Celia, I'm in the doghouse. After I bought the flowers there was a little money left over, so—I hope you don't mind—I had a Coke with some Italian girls I met. When I got back there was frightful umbrage, Mum behaved as if I'd lumbered myself with a shameful bundle in a shawl."

"I'm in the doghouse too. Drunk and disorderly."

"I know. Mum said you'd taken to drink because you couldn't get a man, and Major Gatling said you didn't belong to 'our class', and Mr. Monk said you interested him because you were very withdrawn and had an identity problem. What did happen?''

"Someone doped my drink."

"Goodness. Why?"

Celia was feeling too exhausted to answer this question at sufficient length to do it justice. "It's rather complicated, I'll tell you all about it in the morning. I suppose you could call it a case of mistaken identity in reverse."

"It sounds awful, what can you do about it? Can I help somehow?"

"Bless you, Jane, and listen carefully because as a matter of fact, yes you can."

❦ THREE ❦

Celia's bedroom door was ajar. She had been up since half-past seven, keeping watch on the corridor through the crack. But it was almost eight o'clock before the Hansons went past on their way down to breakfast. As soon as they were safely in the lift, she ran down the stairs to the next floor, rapped on Jane's door, and hurried on downstairs to breakfast.

This feat of organization made it appear to the uninitiated that she and Jane had happened to arrive in the dining-room just after the Hansons, and had decided independently to sit with them at breakfast. Mrs. Hanson ignored Celia, but thanked Jane again for the flowers she had bought for her, and inquired graciously about her progress through the educational system. While Jane was explaining that she would be starting at Oxford in the autumn, the two ladies from Cheshire sat down opposite Celia, and the Armstrong parents arrived to protect Jane from the contaminating influences of Celia the alcoholic and Mrs. Hanson the kleptomaniac.

Now that the audience was large enough, the carefully prepared cross-talk act could begin. Celia brought out a round silver box, inlaid with enamel and gold, which normally contained make-up, and laid it beside her plate.

"Saccharine?" asked Jane according to plan.

"No, just some pills I have to take," said Celia, picking out a digestive tablet she did not need and swallowing it.

Jane produced the next line of the script. "What a pretty box."

"Yes, I got it in Delhi last year, on my way through to Nepal."

"Oh, lucky you!" chipped in one of the ladies from Cheshire. "We've always wanted to go there, haven't we, Anne? Which agency did you go with?"

Celia explained that she had not gone on a package tour, but had spent the whole summer there on a plant collecting expedition. At this point, the audience reaction made the rest of Jane's prepared script unnecessary. The two ladies put eager questions, and Colonel Armstrong, who turned out to have plant-hunted in Sikkim, ignored his wife's sentence of excommunication against Celia and compared notes. Her spirited account of her travels and the rare plants she had seen owed nothing to fiction. She had made the expedition she was describing, ten years ago with Roger.

The Hansons listened in silence as she rammed home the message she had to get across to them: that she had been away from England for the whole of the previous summer and could not possibly be the person Ethel Hanson thought she was. Did they believe her? Edward had half turned to his wife with an expression which might mean "There—I told you you were wrong." Ethel's face with its discontented mouth remained wooden, as if she was not convinced. Celia was far from reassured. Even if they believed her, how quickly would they pass on the message to "them"? She had no wish to be pushed under a car or otherwise disposed of during the day's expedition.

When breakfast was over and Farthingale Tours was leaving the dining-room, Jane stayed behind for a word with Celia. "Do tell me what all this is about."

Before Celia could answer, Mrs. Armstrong called from the doorway. "Jane dear, you really must come and write those postcards before the coach leaves."

Her expression made it clear that this was a well-bred way of saying: "You are to have nothing more to do with that disgusting alcoholic."

"You'd better go, we'll talk in the coach," Celia murmured.

But Mrs. Armstrong's vigilance made this impossible. Jane was shepherded into a window seat beside her father and Farthingale Tours set off towards its first stop of the morning, at the tourist-ridden village of Collodi.

A shock awaited Celia as the coach pulled into its enormous carpark. The two black men who had haunted the party on the previous day were there again, waiting beside a clapped-out Fiat. This time there was no question of coincidence. Collodi was in the foothills above Lucca, and more than fifty miles from Florence. The Fiat had not followed the coach, it was there when they arrived. That meant advance knowledge of the Farthingale Tours itinerary.

The two men must be connected somehow with the South African scenario that the Hansons were involved in. Their arrival on the scene strengthened Celia's resolve to keep herself surrounded with people, as the best way of frustrating any further attack. Her pariah status, and the need to avoid people she suspected of being "them", limited her choice of protectors. But she managed to attach herself loosely to a largely female group centered on the Cheshire ladies and the lugubrious woman in black. With this not very adequate escort, she walked up the village street between shops selling nothing but Pinocchio puppets in various sizes, for Collodi was where the puppet had been invented and the cycle of children's stories about it written. This was one of the reasons why the village was tourist ridden. The other was the spectacular garden of the Villa Garzoni, which attracted millions of visitors every year. That was what Farthingale Tours had come to see.

The garden was on such a grand scale that whoever designed it must have been slightly mad. Its huge parterre was filled with geometrical patterns in carpet bedding and box trees tormented into strange animal shapes. It was also fraught with danger, for the two black men had followed them into the garden and were standing a few yards away. As before, they avoided having their pictures taken, and tagged along as Professor Winkworth led his charges into an open-air theatre with wings and footlights cut from clipped box and statues on its grass stage representing the Muses of Comedy and Tragedy. While he delivered a lecture on Theatre and the Italian Garden, they hovered on the edge of the group, then began what looked like an elaborate game of hide-and-seek. As Farthingale Tours climbed the steps to the upper terraces, the two shadowers were suddenly above them, looking down intently at them over the balustrade. Half-way up a grand water staircase with a statue of Fame at the top, they emerged from a path through the woods to confront the group.

By now others besides Celia had noticed them. "They're the two who followed us yesterday," said Mrs. Enderby-Scott in a frightened voice.

Voices were raised in agreement and the furore became general. What did it mean? Why were they being shadowed in this sly, threatening way?

"Do something, Teddy," urged Mrs. Armstrong. "Ask them what they think they're up to."

After more hide-and-seek, the Colonel cornered them in a labyrinth of clipped box. "I say, you there. Why are you following us?"

They smiled, showing two sets of perfect, rather formidable teeth. "We're not follering you. We paid our entrance fee, we got as much right as you have to be here. So you mind your own business, man, and we'll mind ours."

The smiles became fixed grimaces of confrontation.

"Ignore them," said Mrs. Armstrong. "It's the only way to put people like that in their place."

From then on, the men refused to be shaken off. They followed the party into a bathing pavilion with separate pools for men and women and a room for a hidden orchestra, in a silent persecution which went on for the rest of the visit.

Celia had become less afraid for herself, having decided that to attack her with the whole party looking on would create more problems for ''them'' than it would solve. But the behavior of the two shadowers had set Farthingale Tours cackling in alarm like a flock of geese who had seen a fox, she could not in decency keep quiet any longer. The behavior of this sinister pair must be connected somehow with the Hanson problem. Professor Winkworth would have to be told the whole story. But she would have to get him to herself. Fortunately the second garden on the morning's program was a private one where their two persecutors would not be admitted to cause further panic. If she cornered the Professor during the lunch stop, that would be time enough.

Rather later than planned, the coach pulled out of the carpark. ''Our next stop,'' said Professor Winkworth into his microphone, ''will be at the Villa Salvadori, a few miles from here. I'm afraid its garden will be something of a lucky dip. I didn't manage to see it when I was here last autumn. No one answered the bell at the gate lodge, and there were noisy and intimidating guard dogs loose in the grounds. The villa's owners are in the diplomatic service and live most of the year in Rio de Janerio. But I have had a charming letter from them. They are very sorry that they won't be there to receive us, they don't arrive for the summer till mid-July. But they've given instructions to the caretakers for us to be admitted. According to the authorities, there's a fine *giardino segreto*, an open-air theatre and various other interesting features, but I have no idea what state the place is in now, we shall just have to see.''

In due course the coach drew up outside a pair of solid wooden gates twelve feet high with spikes along the top. This was the forbidding entrance to the Villa Salvadori. The

Professor rang the bell, and set the guard dogs inside barking furiously. Presently a small door in the main gate was opened and the caretaker, a sour-faced, youngish woman in black, peered out. She seemed far from pleased to see them, and made the Professor show her his letter from the owners before she stood aside and let Farthingale Tours file through the little door into the formal courtyard in front of the house.

Their arrival set off another outburst of barking from the guard dogs, shut up in one of the buildings which flanked the courtyard to either side. The Professor raised his voice above the hubbub and tried to exert his charm on the dour house-keeper, but she did not melt. Apart from discovering that her name was Emilia, he made no headway, but was subjected to fierce instructions about the way Farthingale Tours were to conduct themselves while on the premises. Toning down the fierceness as far as possible, the Professor addressed the company in a high-pitched shout to compete with the dogs.

"Emilia here has very kindly consented to show us around, but she is very anxious that we should keep together during our visit, and not wander off on our own. The villa has suffered a lot from the attentions of burglars, which is why the grounds are patrolled by guard dogs. They have been shut up for our benefit, but anyone seen wandering alone is liable to be challenged and perhaps roughly treated by the gardeners. However, we are to be shown the interior first, so let us go in."

The Villa Salvadori had a fortified tower at its centre, surrounded by a two-storey classical building added on by later generations. Emilia took the party on a guided tour. The rooms were very grand, but the painted ceilings with their tumbling goddesses and cupids were cracked and the gilding had tarnished and crumbled. The furniture consisted of second-rate pieces brought down, Emilia explained, from less public rooms upstairs to replace valuable items stolen in the succession of burglaries. A bed allegedly slept in by

Napoleon Bonaparte had been left behind, presumably because it was too heavy to remove, but its hangings were dirty and in tatters. Everything suggested that the place was a frightful problem to its owners, who probably preferred to forget it except for a few weeks in the summer, when they made themselves as comfortable as they could in whichever attics had the least leaky roofs.

Emilia had hurried them from room to room, as if anxious to get the visit over as quickly as possible. As soon as she decently could she herded them out on to the terrace on the garden side of the house. Steps led down from it to a huge lawn, sloping down to a lake. But the grass on the lawn was a foot high, and the neglected hedges to either side had grown forward so much that the statues placed against them at intervals were imbedded in fresh greenery. The same neglect was to be seen everywhere. An elaborate lemon garden was full of weeds which had been sprayed but not removed. The box edgings of the beds in the parterre needed clipping and nothing had been planted in the beds. But Celia decided that this was not the neglect of years: it would take only a few months for an untended garden to get into this state.

The Professor was asking Emilia about the history of the garden, and relaying the answers to the party. But her answers were reluctant and meager, and a helicopter passing overhead made it difficult to hear what he was saying. She was still intent on herding them along, clapping her hands to reprove stragglers and make them rejoin the party as she hurried them round the buildings in the park: a charming rococo *casina* for summer picnics, a grotto with a statue of Venus, a Greek temple which was locked and alleged to have nothing of interest inside it.

From a path through rough woodland, Celia spotted an elegant little tree with glossy dark green leaves. "I believe it's a Lebanon oak," she said, and left the path for a closer look.

Emilia's reaction was immediate and sharp. An angry

shout and an urgent gesture ordered her back to the path. She obeyed, but not before she had been brought up short by a puzzling sight: a wire, stretched between two tree trunks at knee height, between her and the Lebanon oak.

Wondering about this, she moved on with the others. A clearing in the woodland contained an open-air theatre, with footlights cut in box and a grassed stage surrounded by *commedia dell' arte* statues set against the enclosing hedges. Here, desultory activity prevailed. Three gardeners were at work, mowing the grass and clipping the topiary. When Farthingale Tours appeared and raised its cameras, they stopped working and shouted crossly to Emilia.

"*Vietato fotografare*," she announced suddenly.

"Why? Why is it forbidden?" asked several voices.

Paolo asked her, then explained. "Please, she says it's better if the gardeners don't see you taking photographs."

"Why not, Paolo?"

"She did not say this, but they are afraid, I think, that the owners of the house might see the pictures of the garden in this shocking state. Then they will know that they have lazy gardeners, who do nothing till they are threatened with the summer visit of the family."

"Probably been moonlighting all winter elsewhere," said the editress of the flower-arranging magazine.

The helicopter passed overhead again. "What's it doing?" asked Colonel Armstrong. "Flying over us right down low like that; it's done it twice."

Emilia allowed minimal time for admiration of the open-air theatre, then led the party back to the terrace in front of the house. At the top of the steps she looked back to check for stragglers, and gave a gasp of annoyance. "*Ma che razza di modi son questi*?" she asked harshly, pointing towards the lake.

Everyone turned to look. The Prices had eluded Emilia's vigilance and wandered down to the lake. They were standing on the far side of it looking up the vista towards the house in a sinister tableau, like the wicked governess and her paramour in *The Turn of the Screw*.

"Ha! Wonderful!" cried Nigel Monk in undisguised glee.

"Oh, how very tiresome of them," said the Professor tetchily. Paolo muttered something to rather more violent effect in Italian. Mrs. Armstrong said: "It's outrageous, they ought to be packed off home in disgrace."

"Shot," corrected the flower-arranging lady with relish.

"By a firing squad from the Institute of Floral Art," said Nigel Monk.

The remainder of Farthingale Tours gazed at the delinquent couple with varying degrees of disapproval as Mr. Price raised his camera to photograph the garden front of the house. Emilia clapped her hands and beckoned them back into the fold. But the helicopter was still around. The Prices either did not hear or took no notice.

"Shout, everyone," the Professor suggested. Farthingale Tours responded with a loud, incoherent cry, and beckoned. As the gardeners ran out of the open-air theatre to see what was happening, Mr. Price put away his camera without undue haste. He and his wife began strolling back round the edge of the lake.

Frowning furiously, Emilia watched their progress for a moment, then decided not to wait for them, and shooed the party on to the next attraction. This was a sunken garden the size of a tennis court, below a terrace at the side of the house. An elaborate double staircase led down into it at one end.

"*Giardino segreto*," Emilia announced, leading the party down the staircase.

"Ah, the secret garden," said the Professor.

It was twenty feet below ground level and the side walls were lined with masonry. The bottom was laid out in an elaborate design of box-edged beds and lemon trees in pots. There were weeds everywhere and nothing had been planted in the beds.

"According to the authorities," said the Professor,

"there are hidden fountains in this garden. Yes, look, here's one sunk in the mosaic of the garden path."

The helicopter had come back and was passing overhead in a climax of noise.

"In the seventeenth and eighteenth centuries," the Professor went on, "landowners delighted in playing crude practical jokes on their guests. They would lure them into a garden like this, turn on the hidden fountains and soak them to the skin."

The helicopter had stopped its noise. "It's landed, somewhere quite close," said Colonel Armstrong, as the Professor conjured up a vivid picture of bewigged nymphs and shepherds screaming daintily as they were trapped in the downpour.

"Perhaps Emilia could be persuaded to turn the fountains on for us," he suggested. "That is, when we've withdrawn to a safe distance."

Emilia told him the fountains were no longer in working order. Her tone made it clear that even if they were, she would do no such thing.

Somewhere in the neighborhood, people were shouting. A fusillade of shots cracked through the woods. Colonel Armstrong and Major Gatling looked a question at each other.

"Someone after pigeons or rooks," said one of the Cheshire ladies.

The Colonel looked startled, and choked back an impulse to contradict her.

A doorway in the masonry on the side nearest the house had attracted the Professor's attention. He asked Emilia what it was, and got an even more grudging reply than usual. But it excited him greatly.

"An underground passage," he proclaimed, ignoring the confused shouting which was still going on. "Emilia says it leads from the basement of the villa to the *giardino segreto*. The idea was that when the cold *tramontana* blew from the north, the family could come through the passage and take the air in the shelter of the sunken garden.''

The shouting had died down. A single voice seemed to be giving orders. Then came a sudden, loud explosion.

''I know of only one other passage like this one,'' the Professor went on. ''At the Villa Capponi outside Florence, and that has long since been blocked up.''

Impatient at all this lecturing in English, Emilia moved the party on to the end of the sunken garden opposite the staircase, which was blocked by a grotto with a huge male statue in it, brandishing a trident. ''*Grotta di Nettuno*,'' she announced.

''Ah, the Grotto of Neptune,'' said the Professor.

There was no more noise, but the silence seemed ominous.

''When confronted with a grotto like this,'' said the Professor, ''one is immediately reminded of the enormous influence on the Italian Renaissance mind of the *Metamorphoses* of Ovid. Note how the figure emerges from the rock yet at the same time seems to be part of it . . .''

But unease had spread through the group. Most of his audience was not listening. ''I'm going to see what's happening,'' said Colonel Armstrong.

But before he could move far, three men appeared at the top of the elaborate staircase leading down into the sunken garden. They wore black hoods over their heads which left only small holes for the eyes, and they were armed with long-barrelled guns, which they pointed down over the balustrade at the people below.

The gunman in the middle motioned Colonel Armstrong back. Under the hypnotized gaze of Farthingale Tours, all three advanced down the steps. Fanning out among the lemon trees, they drove Farthingale Tours back silently into the grotto, till they were all crowded into the narrow space round the statue of Neptune.

But with an exception. The Hansons had been picked out and prevented from following the others, like the marked sheep at a sheepdog trail. They were standing in the middle of the sunken garden, with guns at their backs.

After a moment of shocked silence, Mrs. Hanson began to scream. "No! No you bastards, let me go!" she shouted.

Colonel Armstrong thrust his way through the crowd in the grotto to attempt a rescue, but a threatening gesture from the third gunman made him draw back.

"Do something, Edward," Mrs. Hanson shouted to her husband. But there was nothing he could do. He was being frog-marched towards the staircase. Still screaming, she threw herself on the ground, but her captor yanked her to her feet and said: "Come, or I shoot you."

Prodded along with the gun, she stumbled towards the staircase, shouting, "Edward, you coward, how dare you let this happen to me?"

"What d'you want me to do, get us both shot?" he replied.

As the Hansons climbed the staircase with their captors behind them, Emilia rushed out of the Grotto of Neptune, shouting abuse in Italian. At the top of the stairs the leading gunman turned and waved her back. Then he bent down and turned on a tap at the top of the steps. Jets of water spouted from the double staircase, the hidden fountains all over the secret garden began to play. Soaked to the skin, Emilia withdrew to the shelter of the grotto.

The masked gunman addressed Farthingale Tours in a deep bass voice. "You get shot if you come out of there before you hear us take off."

The kidnappers withdrew with their victims. A shocked silence filled the overcrowded Grotto of Neptune, broken only by the pattering sound of water. Mrs. Hanson's screams had faded away into the distance. At first everyone was too dazed to be articulate. Presently there were disjointed exclamations, then suddenly everyone was talking at once. Mrs. Enderby-Scott had collapsed into the arms of her husband, who looked as haggard as she did. Emilia kept up a wail of indignant lamentation. Outside in the sunken garden, the fountains went on dispensing a heavy downpour.

"Ah, there it goes," said Major Gatling as the helicopter roared away overhead. "Now. Who's going to turn off the water so we can get out of here?"

"I will," said Jane at once.

"You'll get soaked," her father warned her.

"I shall take off my dress and run like the wind," said Jane. She stripped, revealing a shapely figure clad only in the minutest of panties, which aroused male admiration and envious female disapproval.

"Well what are you all gaping at?" she demanded, handing her dress to her mother to hold. "Have none of you ever seen a girl in a bikini before?"

She pushed her way out of the grotto and ran the gauntlet of the fountains, to turn off the tap at the top of the steps. The downpour stopped.

"And now we must call the police," said the Professor. "*Emilia, avete il telefono alla villa*? Good. Paolo, will you go and phone?"

"One moment, Paolo," said Colonel Armstrong, and handed him a slip of paper. "Pass this on to them."

"What is it, please?"

"The registration markings on the helicopter," the Colonel told him.

Paolo went to the phone with Emilia, and Farthingale Tours emerged cautiously from the grotto into the soaked garden. "The fountains seem to be in perfect order," said the Professor, "despite what Emilia said. But I suppose that is an inappropriate remark in the circumstances."

Colonel Armstrong approached Major Gatling. "Funny sort of kidnapping, eh? Why use a helicopter? A car would have done."

"Getaway problem?" Major Gatling suggested.

"Here, yes. We've been to a lot of other places where a snatch with a car would have been perfectly sound tactics.

Why do it here? The fancy setting with the fountains and whatnot was quite unnecessary."

"Dramatic, though. Terrorists always enjoy a touch of drama. Good publicity for them, doing it here."

"They waited for the right moment," said the Colonel. "Circled about overhead till we were down in this hole where they'd have no trouble rounding us up. Clever."

"Yes. But what was the point of making the set-up so elaborate?"

To Celia, the answer to that was obvious. The whole thing was unreal, there had been no kidnapping, what had just happened was more like a hectic television commercial for chocolate or motor oil. The Hansons, who were actors, had been hired to play the part of kidnap victims against an exotic setting among fountains and classical statuary, with a helicopter to heighten the dramatic effect. Presently it would turn out to be a publicity stunt.

She followed the others up the double staircase to ground level and gazed out over the sweep of lawn which ran down from the villa to the lake.

"The chopper landed in front of the Greek Temple," said Colonel Armstrong. "You can see the marks in the long grass."

Gatling nodded. "And there's something lying in the grass beyond there, a bit nearer the lake. Can you see what it is?"

"Something the chopper left behind?"

"Why down there? It's a long way beyond where it landed."

Celia remembered now what shock had made her forget: this was no publicity stunt, the Hansons had made it clear that they had been hired to abet some crime. She too had seen the object lying in the grass and a horrid thought struck her. "What happened to Mr. and Mrs. Price? They were down by the lake, remember."

"Probably wandered off into Florence by now," said the Colonel, "or Lucca or Pisa."

"But they would have been half-way back up the slope when all that shooting started," cried Celia. "Where are they now?"

"My God, she's right," said the Colonel. Followed by Celia, he set off down the slope. Apart from the Enderby-Scotts, who still looked grey and shell-shocked, the whole of Farthingale Tours streamed after them.

The Prices were lying on their backs in the grass, with grimaces of pain and astonishment on their faces and neat bullet-holes in their chests. Farthingale Tours gathered round in a horrified half-circle.

"Poor things, they must have tried to interfere," said one of the Cheshire ladies. "So the kidnappers shot them."

The Colonel surveyed the distance between the bodies and the marks in the grass where the helicopter had landed. "No, they were too far away to interfere."

Respect for the dead prevented Celia from remarking that even the meekest band of terrorists would turn nasty on being lectured about its misdemeanours by the Prices from a safe distance. It was the sort of brave, silly thing the Prices would do.

"They're mixed up in this somehow," said Mrs. Armstrong. "What were they doing down there by the lake? They must have known the helicopter was coming and went down there to wait for it."

"My dear Dolly," her husband protested, "why would they do that if the people in the helicopter were going to shoot them?"

"I can't think, but I never cared for the Prices, not our sort at all, and I can't help saying so even though they are dead. How do we know what they got up to when they kept dashing off into Florence?"

Three shotguns lay in the grass near the corpses. The Professor bent down to pick one of them up. "Don't, Professor! Fingerprints!" the Colonel warned him.

"Why did the kidnappers leave them behind?" asked the Professor.

"They didn't, they were armed with rifles," the Colonel explained. "The sort you shoot big game with, very odd. The shotguns must belong to the gardeners. Which reminds me, where have they got to?"

Voices from the back of the crowd called for silence. "We think we can hear someone calling for help," said a fat lady who was rumored to be a bishop's widow. Everyone listened. The cries were faint, more like moans than shouts, and they were traced with some difficulty to the Greek Temple. Its doors were shut, but the heavy padlock had been shattered by some kind of explosion, and the door swung open at a push from Major Gatling. Inside, bound, gagged and tied to a pillar, were the villa's three gardeners, still uttering muffled calls for help.

When their gags were removed, all three began talking at once, with the Professor providing a summary in the intervals of their outpourings. They had been working in the open-air theatre, they said, and rushed out when they heard the helicopter arrive. By the time they reached the scene, armed men from the helicopter were shooting at two English tourists who had become separated from the main party. They tried to intervene, but the gunmen overpowered them, then blew open the doors of the Greek Temple and trussed them up inside.

"Why inside the temple?" asked Major Gatling. "Odd, that."

"The whole thing's odd," said the Colonel. "Whoever heard of kidnappers armed with sporting rifles?"

For some time Jane Armstrong had been looking at Celia with an expression of anguished enquiry. Taking advantage of her parents' preoccupation, she slipped past their guard to put the question she had been burning to ask. "Celia, was your 'mistaken identity problem in reverse' something to do with this?"

Celia confirmed that it was, and began telling her the whole story. Meanwhile, an Alfa-Romeo appeared round the corner of the village and sped across the grass, to halt with a squeal of brakes near the scene of the crime. Two uniformed policemen got out and took charge, shepherding everyone away from the two corpses and ignoring a flood of eloquence from the gardeners.

"These are the wrong sort of policemen, very inferior," said Paolo, who had come across the grass from the villa. "But they say, will we please get out of their way and go into the house, and I think it's best if we do what we're told."

"Are those two jokers all we get by way of an investigating team?" asked the Colonel.

"No no no," said Paolo. "Presently will come the *Squadra Mobile* from Pisa, very efficient, who will ask many questions and come to nasty conclusions."

Still in a state of shock, Farthingale Tours straggled back across the grass towards the villa. Mrs. Armstrong was busy laying down the law to the Professor and the policemen and Jane fell into step beside Celia.

"None of this makes sense, Celia. I'm all in a muddle."

"So am I."

"What happened to you was quite weird enough, but what about this kidnapping? Could it be some sort of publicity stunt?"

"That was my first reaction," said Celia. "But does one really shoot two people in cold blood for the sake of publicity? Perhaps, if one's a terrorist advertising a fanatical cause. But a terrorist out for publicity wouldn't be satisfied with kidnapping a stand-in like the Hansons, he'd want a real hostage, a meaty one, famous if possible or at least rich."

"But kidnapping the Hansons must be part of some plan."

"I suppose so, Jane, but what plan?"

"Suppose the real Hansons knew someone wanted to kidnap them, and got these two to stand in for them?"

"Something along those lines perhaps. Very rich people have to think about the kidnapping risk all the time; there are security firms that look after them. It would make sense to hire a pair of broken-down actors as stand-ins, but would they agree? I wouldn't, however badly I needed money, unless the security firm produced squads of bully-boys with shoulder holsters to protect me day and night. There's been no sign of that."

"How about the black bully-boys this morning in the garden?"

Celia considered. "Rather an off-and-on sort of protection, don't you think? They can't even follow us into private gardens like this one. Besides, how could a security firm have discovered that a kidnapping was liable to take place during this particular tour of Italy? And when the Hansons thought I'd recognized them, why didn't they take me aside and say 'Please keep this under your hat, but we're standing in for a couple who . . . et cetera, et cetera' instead of making me drunk and trying to topple me over my balcony? No, I'm afraid that theory's out."

"So what other answer is there?"

"I suppose there could be two lots of people involved," Celia suggested, "one lot frustrating a plan that the other lot are trying to carry out. Or to put it more simply, the kidnapping wasn't part of the plan, it was an attempt to frustrate it."

"Oh yes, Celia, and did you notice? When the kidnapping happened the Enderby-Scotts were terribly upset, much more than anyone else. They would be, if it was their plan that the kidnappers wrecked."

But what was the plan, and why did it have to be wrecked? They had reached the villa, and were racking their brains on the terrace when Mrs. Armstrong summoned Jane brutally inside. The ban on contact with Celia was still in force.

Farthingale Tours had gathered to await events in the grand central hall of the villa. The Professor was wringing his hands in deep distress. "What a dreadful thing to happen. The Prices were by no means my favorites, but without people like them who make frightful nuisances of themselves as a matter of principle, the world would be a poorer place. And we must not forget the Hansons, they will be poorer too, and the kidnappers will be richer; I assume they have been kidnapped for their money. Dear me, we shall be questioned by the police and persecuted by the media, and the tour operator will be very annoyed at so much going wrong, and when one thinks of all the complications it is difficult to feel as keen a sense of personal tragedy as would perhaps be proper, but we must do our best.''

There was plenty to discuss while they waited, and theories were being developed all over the room. The voice of the flower-arranging lady rose above the hubbub. ''Well, we all know who's behind this: those two black brutes who've been making nuisances of themselves.''

This was generally agreed to. ''That's right, they were following us around this morning'' ... ''Yes, and yesterday'' ... ''Of course, it must have been them.''

''It stands to reason,'' argued the flower-arranging lady. ''The Hansons were South African. Typical black terrorist behaviour.''

Jane Armstrong was up in arms at once. ''What makes you think the kidnappers were black? They had hoods over their heads.''

''Their hands were black.''

''No they weren't, they were wearing dark-colored gloves.''

''You're blinded by your left-wing prejudices, my dear. You imagine you saw gloves because that's what you wanted to see.''

Jane appealed to the general company. ''Did anyone else notice their hands?''

Opinion was divided. The flower-arranging lady and the lugubrious woman in black headed a large faction in favor of bare black hands and no gloves. A minority, led by Jane and the elegant bachelor from Norfolk, was equally sure of the opposite. It was a question of political principle rather than factual observation and there were surprisingly few "don't knows". Celia kept her own counsel.

"If they were white they were communists," declared the flower-arranging lady. "Communism and black terrorism, it's all part of the same thing."

"You've no evidence at all for saying that," Jane insisted. "Perhaps the Hansons are liberals. It could be a bit of run-of-the-mill terrorism by the South African government's dirty-tricks department."

"What nonsense, Jane," decreed Mrs. Armstrong. "Who says the Hansons are liberals?"

The question was thrown open to general debate, but the meager evidence could be read either way. According to the alleged bishop's widow, the Hansons had refused to discuss South African politics, saying no outsider could understand them, which sounded like apartheid on the defensive. But Mrs. Hanson had told the Cheshire ladies that she had contributed large sums to starvation relief in Ethiopia and Mozambique, which pointed to liberalism and compassion. The couple in the room next to the Hansons had heard violent quarrels, and suggested that one of them was liberal and the other not.

"There was something very odd about them," volunteered a woman from Shropshire. "For instance, why did she call him 'Jimmy'?"

"Did she?"

"Yes, in the Marchesa's garden yesterday, they were quarreling again and I happened to overhear. She distinctly called him 'Jimmy', but his name's Edward, don't you remember? She was always saying 'Edward, come and look at this'. So why did she call him 'Jimmy'?"

Jimmy. Of course, Celia thought. That's his first name, I remember now. Jane was looking at her, half expecting her to say something. But she had no intention of answering the question. "They" were in the room. Her battle of wits with them was not over. The less she seemed to know about the Hansons and their double identity, the safer she would be.

❦ FOUR ❧

Commissario Ciampi of the Pisa *Squadra Mobile* brooded gloomily as his Alfa-Romeo flashed along the fast lane of the *autostrada* with its headlights blazing. A hostage-taking could make or break a senior detective, depending on what happened. If the terrorists butchered their hostages and dumped them in the boot of a stolen car, he was a failure. If he got them freed without too much publicity about the ransom, he was a resounding success. Ciampi, a specialist in kidnappings among other things, sometimes compared his career with its sickening ups and downs to a trip on a roller-coaster in a fairground.

Fortunately this was not a political case. Having a judge or a politician as the victim gave the proceedings an uncomfortably high profile, with the media snapping at your heels day and night, and a strong probability that the victim would end up dead. In his last case, a Nato general had been killed soon after the snatch. But the kidnappers kept the publicity pot boiling for months by convincing the media that he was still alive. Photographs in which he appeared to be holding the newspaper of the day were produced at regular intervals, and the police laboratory could not come up with cast-iron proof that Ciampi was right to dismiss them as clever fakes. This time it was only a matter of two foreign tourists kidnapped for ransom. But a hostage situation was always a test of nerve, and he was feverish with tension when he arrived to start work at the Villa Salvadori.

Journalists had gathered already outside the forbidding entrance gates under the eyes of the policeman on guard. As he waited for the car to be let through, microphones were thrust at him through the half-open windows. The pressure was building up already.

"Curse it, Giorgio," he growled to his assistant, Sergeant Barbetti. "How do they always find out so soon?"

They both knew the answer: a well-rewarded tip-off from someone in the communications-room at headquarters in Pisa. But Barbetti, a placid blond man running to fat, said nothing. He knew his chief's moods. There were times to keep silent, and this was one of them. He respected Ciampi as a first-class detective, sympathized with him as a deeply insecure man, and considered it part of his duty to try to keep his chief calm.

The car drove through the gates and over the grass on the garden side of the house to the scene of the crime. The usual people were already there and Ciampi, forcing himself to sound calm and relaxed, listened to their reports. There had been a murder as well as a kidnapping. Two English tourists had been shot, each with a single bullet from a rifle or machine carbine. Three shotguns, belonging to three gardeners who had witnessed the killing, had been found beside the bodies. The kidnapping had taken place elsewhere, and the group of tourists who had witnessed that were inside the villa, waiting to be questioned.

"How many?" Ciampi asked.

"Twenty-five, perhaps thirty, *Signor Commissario*."

"Too many, I will leave them till later. Where are the gardeners?"

"Over there, *Signor Commissario*. Enrico and Giovanni Fabbri and Luigi Cardini. The Fabbris are father and son, and Cardini is a cousin."

The gardeners were standing a little apart, wearing nervous scowls which deepened as Ciampi approached them. They told how they had rushed out of the open-air theatre when they heard the helicopter land, but had not been in time to prevent the shooting of the two tourists and had been overpowered and trussed up in the Greek Temple.

The story came out awkwardly, as if they were uneasy about it. Ingrained peasant distrust of the police? Ciampi wondered. Perhaps, but were they hiding something?

"The shotguns which were found beside the bodies are yours?" he asked.

They agreed, grudgingly.

"You are not under suspicion of murder," he told them. "The tourists were killed with bullets from a rifle, not with shot. But there are empty cartridges in all three shotguns. When did you fire them?"

"When we came out of the wood and saw what was happening."

"Without wounding any of the kidnappers?"

They consulted each other mutely. "The range was too great," said the elder Fabbri.

"I see. When you fired, you were standing where?"

Hesitant gestures indicated a spot near where the path from the open-air theatre emerged on to the lawn. Ciampi measured the distance with his eye. It was about a hundred metres from there to the spot where the two tourists were lying. The landing-place of the helicopter was half-way between the two.

"Yet your guns were found in the grass near the two tourists," Ciampi remarked.

"We ran over to see if we could help them," said the elder Fabbri.

They had to be lying. Would the kidnappers let three armed gardeners rush past them and on for fifty metres or so to bend over the corpses? Then catch up with them and overpower them? And there was something else that did not add up.

"Do you always carry your guns with you when you work in the garden?" he asked.

"Not always. Today we were going to shoot little birds in the woods when we had finished work."

"When you heard the helicopter land, you had no reason to expect that it contained armed men who were about to take hostages. Why did you bring your guns with you when you rushed on to the scene?"

Once more, Fabbri was the spokesman. "It is not normal for a helicopter to land in a private park without permission. We suspected that something was wrong." He appealed to the others, who nodded vigorously.

Ciampi abandoned them for the present. He would try to break down their story later, but now, something must be done about the crowd of tourists cooped up in the villa, and he walked over the grass towards it with Sergeant Barbetti.

"Those men are lying, Giorgio," he muttered, stiff with tension, "and I have made a bad mistake. Why, why did I leave them together while they gave their testimony? If I had questioned them separately, there would have been contradictions between their stories."

"I do not think so, *capo*," Barbetti replied. "Before you arrived, they had time to agree what they would say. Moreover, you were not to know that they had anything to hide."

Ciampi's grim face did not relax. "They were standing beside the tourists when the helicopter landed, it is the only way the thing makes sense. But why do they not say so? And why did the two tourists go down to the lake by themselves, instead of remaining with the others who were visiting the secret garden?"

"Are they perhaps not ordinary tourists, *capo*, but something else?"

"If that is so, it might explain why the kidnappers thought it unnecessary to shoot the gardeners who were armed, but necessary to shoot the tourists who were not. But why do the gardeners wish to create a distance in our minds between them and the tourists? That is the key question."

Barbetti disagreed. The key question was, why did the kidnappers think it necessary to blow open the door of the Greek Temple and hustle the gardeners inside? But he did not point this out. His chief would go through torments of guilt and inferiority if he was not left to think of that for himself.

Under the fading goddesses and cupids of the saloon's grand ceiling, Farthingale Tours was getting impatient. A lot was going on at the scene of the crime, but no one had come near them. It was after two o'clock, and Professor Winkworth had long since blurted out what everyone else was thinking. "I suppose it is heartless to be hungry in the presence of death, but I must confess to an occasional pang. Do the police not eat? British ones in detective stories wolf sandwiches at irregular intervals in sordid cafes. One had hoped that Italian police would be different and have their pasta at fixed times, but apparently not."

"Here comes someone," said the Colonel, looking out into the garden. Two men in plain clothes were approaching across the grass, a fine-featured forty-year-old with receding dark hair and a younger man, blond and threatening to run to fat. They came into the room through the glass doors opening on to the terrace and the older of the two addressed the company in excellent English. "Good afternoon, ladies and gentlemen, let me introduce myself. I am Commissario Alessandro Ciampi of the *Squadra Mobile* in Pisa, and Giorgio Barbetti here is, as you might say, my side-kick. Who, please, is the leader of the tour?"

Professor Winkworth identified himself, and the two conferred for a moment. Then Ciampi spoke again. "I shall of course need to take statements from you all, but there is much to be done first. I think it is not necessary to keep you here hanging around, so to speak, and it will be more comfortable for you if you return now to your hotel. Sergeant Barbetti and I will come there to take your statements later this afternoon."

He nodded stiffly and withdrew, leaving them to find

73

their way to the coach, which was waiting outside the gates. But the way to it was blocked by the media, who fell upon Farthingale Tours like a pack of starving wolves. Soon interviews were going on everywhere, with much emphasis on the two sinister blacks who had dogged the tour's footsteps; a significant fact, everyone thought, because the Hansons came from South Africa. As in duty bound, everyone assured the media that the Hansons had been enormously popular travelling companions. Most people were prepared to take the same line about the Prices. But Mrs. Armstrong was not. They were up to no good, she said, and had often gone off by themselves on mysterious errands in Florence.

The media were delighted with this more interesting version, and abandoned the theory that the Prices were nice ordinary people who had been brutally shot down. Elaborating on what had proved to be a popular line of talk, Mrs. Armstrong added that they had refused to let their room be searched, a most suspicious circumstance.

Searched? The media were even more delighted. Why was it necessary to search their room?

Having thus let the cat out of the bag about the theft and reappearance of the Marchesa's cream jug, Mrs. Armstrong hinted that Mrs. Hanson was a kleptomaniac. But this was not a success with the media. Mrs. Hanson was supposed to be the well-liked, innocent victim of a cowardly terrorist attack. She could not be a kleptomaniac at the same time, it blurred the picture and would confuse the public.

A television crew had picked on Jane Armstrong as the only pretty girl available, and had made her give a rather exaggerated picture of how frightened she had been. The Enderby-Scotts, however, had pushed their way past the journalists and climbed into the coach, still looking shaken and very grim.

Having done their duty by the media, Farthingale Tours returned to the hotel, and sat down to a belated and improvised lunch, but Celia went upstairs first to telephone England again. At all costs she must find out the Hansons' real names at once. But there was still no reply from the Claytons, and she remembered now: it was a long holiday weekend in England. The Claytons were probably away from home at some race meeting, for their lives revolved around the horse. There were a few other people in her address book who might know, and she rang them. But two did not reply, one had been away during the festival and another was said by her cleaning woman to be on holiday in Scotland for a week. Celia was in despair. She would have to face the police in an hour or two without knowing the Hansons' names, and the holiday weekend had robbed her of any chance of finding out. Her story would sound so thin and vague that she would be dismissed at once as half crazy. She had suffered that way once before at the hands of the police, and it had left a deep hurt. Fighting down panic, she rang even the unlikeliest people, but without result.

Mrs. Waters was having an afternoon snooze when the telephone rang in her converted loft overlooking the Thames in London's trendy dockland.

"Mrs. Waters? This is Edward Pick of the *Evening Express*."

She yawned. "Yes?"

"I'm right in thinking you're the daughter of Mr. and Mrs. Edward Hanson, who live in Cape Town?"

"Yes. What of it?"

"I have some very distressing news for you. Your parents have been kidnapped."

"Oh my God. How? When?"

"Today. Just after twelve."

Mrs. Waters gathered her wits. "Our time, or Bermuda time?"

"Italian time, I imagine. They're an hour ahead."

"What the hell's Italy got to do with it?"

"Your parents were on a package tour in Tuscany when it happened."

Anger and shock kept Mrs. Waters silent for a moment. "If this is a practical joke, it's in very bad taste."

"No, Mrs. Waters, this is on the level. It's on all the agencies. They were snatched at gunpoint somewhere in Tuscany and taken away in a hijacked helicopter."

"Look here, this is some silly mistake. My parents are perfectly well, I spoke to them on the phone just after lunch."

"But I spoke to their housekeeper in Bermuda just now. She said they weren't there, and gave me your number."

"They wouldn't be, they'd hopped over to Florida to spend a few days with friends."

"Really? Would you give me the phone number of these friends?"

"Certainly not. I'm not having them disturbed with a lot of half-baked gutter-press nonsense."

She put down the phone, but it rang again almost at once, with the same enquiry from another paper.

When the same thing happened a third time, she rang her husband, who was a City whiz-kid, at work and told him to find some way of putting a stop to this nuisance.

Stock Exchange whiz-kids are paid to be decisive, and Henry Waters was no exception. "Ring Scotland Yard, ask to speak to the Anti-Terrorist Squad, and tell them what you've just told me. There's obviously been a mix-up, they can sort it out."

"But can they stop the media from phoning me?"

"Goodness knows, but do ring them at once. Whoever's been kidnapped in mistake for your parents is liable to get hurt."

"Can't you phone them?"

"No, they'll want to talk to you anyway and I've got Tokyo waiting on the other line."

Grumbling, Mrs. Waters did as she was told, and was put through to Inspector Tomlinson of the Anti-Terrorist Squad.

"I see, madam," he said after listening to her recital.

"I'll send a telex straight away to our colleagues in Italy, telling them what you say. As a matter of form, perhaps you'll give me the number of the friends your parents are staying with, so that I can check."

"Very well, but can you stop the media from making nuisances of themselves on the telephone?"

"I'm afraid not, but is there by any chance an answering machine on your phone?"

"Naturally, most people have one, don't they? Why?"

"If you put it on, you won't have to accept any calls you don't want."

When he had got her off the phone, he checked that Mr. and Mrs. Hanson were indeed at the Florida number she had given him, and drafted a telex to Rome. Not that it was really necessary, the media would be on to this like a flash. He was sorry for his Italian colleagues, they would have a very tricky situation to deal with. The Italian radio and television would pick up the story at once, and the hostage-takers would know they had got the wrong couple. How would they react? Release their hostages at once? Or kill them, rather than let them loose to tell their story to the media and make their captors the laughing-stock of the Italian terrorist underground? It depended on who the kidnappers were, and what mood they were in when they got the news. And that was something that the police team dealing with them could not hope to know. But it was not his case, thank goodness.

At the Villa Salvadori the investigating team had discovered an elaborate system of trip-wires, extending through the woods around the villa. The wires were at knee height, and connected to an alarm system. According to Emilia Strozzi, they were a defense against burglary, to supplement the guard dogs. Were such elaborate defences really necessary, Ciampi asked her, now that almost all the valuables in the villa had been stolen? Yes, said Emilia, the burglaries had made her nervous. Would-be burglars did not necessarily know that there was nothing valuable left for them to steal. She was afraid of being murdered in her bed.

The discovery of the trip-wires delayed Ciampi at the scene of the crime for longer than he intended, and it was late afternoon before he and Barbetti reached the hotel in Montecatini Terme. His first concern was to search the Hansons' room, looking for an address book, or for any document which would give him a lead to their relatives. He must contact the family at once before the hostage-takers got at them, and block any attempt to pay a ransom. In all probability a kidnap insurance firm was involved. In that case he would have to deal with an insurance adjuster who would do his best to bypass the police and negotiate secretly with the kidnappers on behalf of the family. The thought of such underhand dealings behind his back infuriated him.

The Hansons' bedroom was a disappointment. It contained no personal papers of any kind, only their return tickets from London and some travel literature. Even their passports were missing, no doubt they had them on them when they were kidnapped. Though South African, they bought their clothes in Europe, to judge from the designer labels in her few dresses, and the one in his only formal suit. They seemed to have brought the bare minimum of possessions with them on holiday, and had left nothing behind which gave a clue to their background.

Had they said anything to their fellow-tourists which would help to locate their family? That question, among others, would have to be asked. He went downstairs, to find Farthingale Tours handing over rolls of exposed film to Barbetti. There would certainly be some photos of the Hansons among their holiday snaps. They were needed urgently for circulation to the press, and the same applied to photos of the mysterious Price couple. The films would be developed in the police laboratory at Pisa, and returned to their owners.

Ciampi and Barbetti settled down in the little writing-room of the hotel, to question the tourists one by one.

Professor Winkworth, the first witness, seemed to have only a dim perception of realities outside his specialist field of the Italian Renaissance. Apart from a confused story about a stolen cream jug, his only useful contribution was a crumpled typewritten list of the people on the tour, which he produced from a bulging brief case.

When he had gone, Ciampi handed the list to Barbetti. "The names are in alphabetical order, Giorgio. Let us follow the same system and talk first to Colonel Armstrong."

The Colonel did not know of "any relative or connection of the kidnapped couple whom we should inform about their situation". But he proved to be an excellent witness, precise about times and with a soldier's ability to distinguish between different types of gunfire. "There was a lot of shouting after the chopper landed, then a burst of shooting, some of it from shotguns and some from rifles. A minute or so later there was an explosion, as if someone was trying to demolish something."

Ciampi nodded, "They demolished the padlock on the door of a small building, which I believe is called the Greek Temple. After the explosion, what?"

"Quite a pause. I suppose they were getting those gardener chaps into the little building and tying them up."

He estimated that about three minutes had passed before the kidnappers appeared in the sunken garden. Asked to describe them, he gave a detailed account of what they were wearing, and said he thought they were black, linking this with a mention of the two blacks whose sinister presence had so disturbed Farthingale Tours in the hours before the hold-up.

"And the kidnappers were armed with what? Carbines, perhaps?"

"No. That was what surprised me. They were sporting guns. Big-game rifles, in fact."

"Big-game rifles? You cannot be serious."

"I'm perfectly serious. At first I thought it was some

kind of joke; in fact I still would if the Prices hadn't got written off, poor things.''

When he had gone Ciampi and Barbetti exchanged looks. ''He is right,'' Barbetti exclaimed. ''To kidnap with sporting guns is not terrorism, it is farcical!''

''But the actors in this farce are also murderers,'' said Ciampi.

''Perhaps the Colonel is mistaken, *capo.*''

''A soldier does not make mistakes about guns, Giorgio. No, there is something twisted here, it lacks the clarity of terrorism. I do not like this case.''

Their next witness was Mrs. Armstrong, who agreed with her husband that the kidnappers were black, but seemed most concerned to convince Ciampi that the Prices were up to no good and that their breakaway visits to Florence had some sinister purpose. She was followed by her daughter, who insisted that the kidnappers were white. Apart from that she contributed nothing, but gladdened the two policemen's hearts by being very pretty. Miss Burton from Suffolk, who followed, was middle-aged and not pretty, and the next witness, the Contessa Carstairs from Hampshire, was even worse, a white-faced female clown who was a real pain to look at and talked nonsense at great length.

She was followed by a Mr. Enderby-Scott, who seemed very ill at ease and said that his wife was too shocked to make a statement. He claimed to know nothing about firearms, and added nothing to Ciampi's knowledge. Of the next three witnesses one thought the kidnappers were white, another was a ''don't know'', and the third, a Major Gatling from Berkshire, said black. All three insisted on giving a dramatic account of the shadowing by the two black bullyboys. Nobody remembered the Hansons saying anything about their family.

Questioned about the firearms carried by the terrorists, Major Gatling agreed with the Colonel that they were big-game rifles. But his evidence on that point carried less weight because he had obviously compared notes with the Colonel.

"Who do we take next, Giorgio?" the Commissioner asked with a sigh.

Barbetti consulted the typed Farthingale Tours list. "The Signorina Grant, *capo*. From Devon."

"Call her. Let us hope that she is young and pretty and less talkative than the terrible Carstairs."

The tiny woman whom Barbetti ushered into the room was not young, though she had a youthful figure and complexion. Her hair had gone prematurely white, and for some extraordinary reason she had omitted to dye it.

"You are the Signorina Grant from Devon?" Ciampi asked.

"No, I am the Signora Grant from Sussex."

"But—" An eloquent gesture appealed to the typewritten list.

Celia had decided to keep the outline simple. "Miss Grant from Devon is my sister-in-law. She was prevented from coming on the tour at the last moment, and I substituted for her. That was after the list was typed."

Ciampi embarked on his routine list of questions.

"The kidnappers were white," she said firmly. "They wore brown gloves and their faces were covered with hoods, leaving only slits for the eyes. But one of them had a gap between the bottom of his hood and his bomber jacket, and he was definitely white."

"Could it not be a white scarf, Signora, that you saw?"

"No, when I say white, I mean the normal colour of European flesh. On this question of colour, I imagine other witnesses have mentioned to you the two black men who have been following the tour. I hope you won't attach too much importance to them, because their behavior was quite ridiculous, they were deliberately drawing attention to themselves in order to mislead. They were sent after us to plant in our minds the idea that this was a Black Power hostage-taking, when in fact it is nothing of the kind."

Barbetti was horrified. This doll-like creature was presuming to tell his chief what to think. He would not like that. And to make her offense even worse, she was talking sense. If the kidnapping was indeed a sinister farce of some kind, the two men could well be walkers-on in it.

Ciampi looked daggers at her, and put his next question. Had the Hansons mentioned to her any relative whom the police ought to contact?

Celia was desperate. She had rung the Claytons again five minutes ago, but there was still no reply. Nevertheless, she plunged in. "They aren't rich, they aren't resident in South Africa, and I don't think their name's Hanson."

Told in cold blood, the story sounded wildly improbable. When she had finished there was a significant pause. She could see from their faces that her rating as a witness had slumped heavily.

"You are telling us," said Ciampi icily, "that Edward and Ethel Hanson are not at all Edward and Ethel Hanson, but two semi-starving actors whom you met for a few minutes a year ago?"

"Not just a few minutes. Longer."

"And you do not know their names?"

"No. I did, but I've forgotten them. I've been ringing people in England all afternoon trying to find out, but it's a public holiday there and no one's at home to answer."

The two policemen exchanged glances. This lady, they concluded, is completely mad.

Why, oh why didn't I keep quiet? Celia thought. All her old fear of the police had come surging back. It dated from the time, several years ago, when she had been right and the police wrong, but this had only come to light after the whole village had sent her to Coventry as a mad woman.*

Her hands were twisted together in her lap, and Ciampi was staring at them. Panicking blindly, she decided that he

*See *Green Trigger Fingers* by the same author.

was wondering why she wore no wedding-ring. Busy on the phone to England, she had forgotten to put it on again.

"I took it off," she stammered, "because I didn't want the Hansons to recognize me, so I let everyone on the tour think I was a Miss Grant from Devon."

Ciampi saw no reason to believe this. An aging woman had removed her ring in the hope of a last holiday love-affair, but her wild manner had probably frightened the men off.

"No doubt you had your reasons for removing your ring," he said coldly.

Plunging on, she began to tell him about the Marchesa's stolen jug, but he cut her short. "We have already heard of this from the Professore Winkworth."

"But you don't know what I overheard the Hansons say, or what happened afterwards at the dinner-table." She told the story, very badly, and added: "I can tell you exactly who was at the table at the time."

Instead of taking up this offer, Ciampi asked her if she had communicated her theories to her fellow-tourists. "Of course not, you haven't taken in what I've been saying. One of them, perhaps two, are involved in whatever mischief the Hansons were up to. If they knew what I've just told you, I'd be in very serious danger."

When she had gone, Ciampi let out a "puah!" of relief.

"Completely mad," said Barbetti.

"Yes. Persecution mania, poor woman. Who is next?"

The first person Celia ran into in the lounge after this shaming encounter was Nigel Monk, who amused himself by putting on a show of tender psychiatric concern. "Celia, you look dreadful," he said in a mock-funeral voice. "Are you horribly, appallingly upset?"

"I'm perfectly OK, thank you."

"You aren't, you know. We've all had a shock, but it must have been much worse for a real sensitive like you. Try to relax more, let your emotions come out, or you'll be heading for serious trouble. Keeping up a brave front is taking too much out of you.''

''There's nothing wrong with me,'' said Celia.

''Oh but there is, you know. You're heading for a nervous breakdown.''

''Then for goodness sake let me have it in peace.''

He was grinning. Furious, she dodged past him to take refuge in her room.

When she had recovered a little, she rang the Claytons again. There was still no reply. Desperate, she was about to try one of the other numbers when there was a knock on her door.

''Who's there?''

''Jane. Are you all right, Celia?''

''Yes,'' said Celia untruthfully as she let her in. ''What made you think I wasn't?''

''You looked awful when you came out from talking to those policemen. What happened? Didn't they believe you?''

''No, and they thought I was half mad. Don't you?''

''Of course not, Celia. But I'm still very puzzled. How do the Prices fit in?''

Celia collected her wits. ''I've been wondering about that. Why were they the ones who got killed? Shooting the gardeners would have made much more sense, they were armed.''

''Perhaps the Prices knew something. They went down to the lake so that they could meet the helicopter when it arrived.''

''If they were in on the kidnapping, why did the people in the helicopter shoot them? If they weren't, and intended to frustrate the kidnapping somehow, why didn't they take guns with them? They must have been expecting trouble. No, it's much likelier that they're an innocent pair of nuisances who went down to the lake out of normal Price cussedness and ran into trouble.''

"In which case we're back at 'why did they get shot?'" Jane said. "It doesn't make sense."

"They probably fit in somehow, they were the ones who told everyone that I wasn't Miss Grant from Devon and started me on the downward path to the doghouse. That could have been a deliberate attempt to undermine my credibility, so that no one would believe me if I said the Hansons weren't what they pretended to be. On the other hand, showing up my giddy masquerade was the sort of thing they'd do anyway, typically awkward Price behavior. Anyway they can't be the Hansons' minders, they weren't at the dinner-table when Mrs. Hanson made her announcement about the Marchesa's jug."

"I suppose not. Which of them was she talking to when she made that scene?"

"Goodness knows. She thinks and speaks of these people she's involved with as 'they' and 'them', which seems to point to a couple. I think we can rule out your parents—"

"I suppose we must," said Jane. "Their mentality is basically criminal, in the sense that they're fascists. But if they were going in for anything devious, observant little Jane who asks awkward questions wouldn't have been brought along."

"There's something very odd about the Enderby-Scotts," said Celia.

"I think it's only that they're ultra-shy. How about the dreadful old woman with the stepson?"

"Is he a stepson? His name's George Johnson. He could be, if she was divorced from a man called Johnson who had a child by his next wife. But it doesn't follow."

"Why? What else could he be, Celia?"

When Celia enlightened her she looked shocked. "I don't believe it. She's *old*. They *couldn't*."

"I know it's difficult for anyone your age to believe it, but it does happen."

"Ugh. How nasty, it doesn't bear thinking about. My money's on Major Gatling. Dad says he's spooky."

"Spooky?" Celia echoed. "In what way?"

"Sorry. Army slang. He seems to know a lot of high-ups, generals and so on, by their first names, but what he says about his military career doesn't add up, Dad says. That usually means MI5 or MI6 or some other undercover set-up, for which the accepted expression is 'spooky'."

"He may have been spooky once, but at present he seems to have other things on his mind."

"Oh. You mean his sex problem."

"My poor Jane, have you suffered from his attentions too?"

"I think most of the women have to some extent."

"That doesn't rule him out necessarily. Pretending to be a rampant *kniphofia* would be quite a good cover."

"Pretending to be a what?"

"Sorry. Gardening slang. *Kniphofia* is the botanical name for a red-hot poker. What d'you make of Nigel Monk?"

"He's the joker in the pack, and most of his jokes are nasty enough to make him a criminal."

"Then there's the Professor," said Celia. "But if he tried to commit a crime the whole tour would have to turn to and sort out the muddle he'd made. I've just realized, though, that if there are a lot of conspirators only one of them would have to be sitting at the table with us. The other could be anyone, even Paolo, the courier."

"Oh, I refuse to suspect him, he's nice," said Jane. "He told me right off that he had a steady girlfriend. Not that I go for goo-goo eyes and Latin ringlets, but it was nice of him to warn me in case."

"The trouble about this is, we're following irrational hunches. We haven't really eliminated anyone."

"No, but we can if we keep our ears open," said Jane. "I think we should chat up all the suspects and see what we come up with."

This suggestion gave a big boost to Celia's morale. "What a good idea. Being a lame duck in a doghouse will handicap me a bit, but I'll do my best. Who will you tackle?''

"Any of them except Major Gatling, whose nymphet I am not prepared to be.''

"Start with George, why don't you? If necessary you could simulate an unrequited passion.''

"Why not? His nicotiney fingers are off-putting but yes, what fun.''

"Oh dear, you're like me,'' said Celia. "When anything sinister like this happens I simply have to know. Isn't it awful?''

"Awful, but exciting.''

❦ FIVE ❦

It was shortly after four o'clock, London time, when Mrs. Waters returned from walking her Pekinese and listened to the contents of her answering machine. Most of the messages were frantic appeals from the media to ring them back. But there was also one from a man who spoke in a harsh bass growl. "Now you listen carefully, Mrs. Waters. You want to see your mother and father alive, right? You don't want them to come to no harm. So you switch off this fucking awful machine and talk to me. I'll ring you every hour at the hour, three, four, five, six, seven, eight, nine, ten, eleven, twelve. If you still won't speak, if you're still hiding behind your fucking awful machine, then we cut off your mum's and your dad's ears and we post them to you, so do be sensible. 'Bye now."

On recovering from her shock and anger, Mrs. Waters rang her contact at Scotland Yard, Inspector Tomlinson. "Look here, Inspector, a man using filthy language has had the impertinence to leave a message on my answering machine."

"I'm afraid obscene phone calls aren't in my province, Mrs. Waters. Your local police station will deal with it."

"But he says he'll cut off mum's and dad's ears if I don't talk to him."

After a moment of astonished silence Tomlinson said: "Really? Then that is my province. But what a very surprising development."

"Yes. These moronic kidnappers have made the same mistake as the media."

"Could you play the message over to me?" Tomlinson asked.

"Oh dear. How?"

"Hold the ear-piece near the machine and make it play the message."

"Very well, but why are they bothering me? If anyone's going to pay a ransom, it's the relatives of this other couple. Surely these idiotic kidnappers know they've boobed?"

"Not necessarily. The story's been on the media here, of course, but the Italian radio and TV may not have picked it up yet."

"So you say, but it's a damn nuisance."

"I'm sure it is, Mrs. Waters, but could you play me the message?"

After a lot of grumbling, Mrs. Waters did as she was told.

Inspector Tomlinson thought for a moment. Surely the hostages must have told their captors that they had got the wrong couple? But perhaps they had not been given the chance, or alternatively the kidnappers might have refused to believe them. "I shall come round if I may," he said, "and bring some special recording equipment with me. It's possible that they'll ring again before they discover their mistake. If so, we'd like you to keep the caller talking for as long as possible. And meanwhile, don't wipe the message on your answering machine, will you?"

"Oh. I was just going to. Would you rather I didn't?"

"Please don't. I'll be with you as soon as I can."

By ten to six he was sitting with her beside the telephone in her trendy riverside apartment. Also in the room was a

Special Branch technician who had copied the kidnapper's message from her answering machine on to equipment he had brought with him. Tomlinson was almost sure that the hoarse bass voice and Afro accent were a disguise.

It was almost six o'clock, when the kidnapper was due to make his next attempt to get past her answering machine. When he rang, Mrs. Waters was supposed to try to keep him on the line as long as possible while a battery of electronic equipment at the exchange tried to trace the call.

But would he ring? Surely by now the kidnappers must have absorbed what the media were telling them and realized that they had got the wrong Hansons? But who had they got instead? Another pair of fat cats, good for a ransom? Tomlinson hoped not. Once they were convinced that their victims were not ransom material, there would be no point in holding on to them. What happened after that would depend on the hostages themselves. If they had been sensible and tried to build up a relationship with their captors, they had a good chance of being released. But if they had got stroppy, the kidnappers would have got stroppy too, and might kill them in a fit of temper. They were obviously quite capable of it, having already killed two bystanders at the scene of the snatch.

The telephone rang. "Steady now, Mrs. Waters," said Tomlinson.

She braced herself for action, then picked it up. "Hullo, Ann Waters speaking."

"Oh good, you bein' sensible now," said the hoarse, slow voice. "That machine ain't no good, it make us very angry. Now listen carefully what I tell you. Your parents got a lot of money and we want some. We want a million pounds."

"Well you can go on wanting it."

"Don't be fuckin' stupid, Mrs. Waters, that sort of talk ain't no good. You fond of your parents, ain't you? Don't want them to come to no harm?"

"They aren't going to come to any harm."

"Don't you be so sure of that, Mrs. Waters. You don't do what we want, then we can be very nasty."

"Nothing could make you nastier than you are already," she said, to Tomlinson's alarm. He signed to her to cool it. There was no point in getting the man angry and overexcited.

"Listen now, Mrs. Waters," said the deep, grainy voice. "Racists like you don't like having to contribute to the cause of oppressed black South Africa, we know that. Just don't you be rude now, you listen quietly."

"No, you listen to me. My parents are on the other side of the Atlantic, quite safe. You aren't even competent enough to kidnap the right people. God knows who the couple are that you've got hold of, but they must be hopping mad at you."

"Don't tell me such lies, Mrs. fuckin' awful Waters."

Mrs. Waters went scarlet with anger. "If you're going to use filthy language I shall put the phone down."

Predictably, this provoked a torrent of obscenity from the other end. Tomlinson snatched the phone from her before she could put it down. "Police here, Inspector Tomlinson speaking. Good evening."

"I don't want to talk to no policeman."

"I just want to tell you that what Mrs. Waters says is quite correct, please don't do anything silly. We're satisfied that the people you're holding are not Mr. and Mrs. Hanson."

"If that's right and she's got nuttin' to worry about, why's she got police in her house? It's all lies. You tell her she better think it over and we ring her again tomorrow. 'Bye now."

Later, the specialists at the exchange reported that the call had come through the international exchange. It had been cut off before they could trace it further.

Ciampi and Barbetti had finished questioning Farthingale Tours. Ciampi went back to headquarters to draft a long telex of enquiries about the Hansons, and send it off to the Anti-Terrorist Squad in London, leaving Barbetti to do the one job still outstanding at the hotel: a search of the Prices' bedroom.

According to the other tourists, the Prices had become hysterically defensive at the very suggestion that their room might be searched. But the only thing Barbetti found which might have accounted for this was a bottle of duty-free whisky hidden in the wardrobe. Were they then alcoholics? Probably not, the bottle was three-quarters full. They must have bought it in the aircraft and drunk out of their tooth glasses instead of being sociable and paying more for their drinks at the hotel bar. But everyone knew that the English were misanthropical and very mean.

The Prices' other possessions included vitamin and yeast tablets, a packet of wholefood biscuits, Italian phrasebooks and guides to Florence and Lucca, and what seemed to Barbetti an unnecessary quantity of unfashionable peasant-style women's clothes. But where were their passports, which had not been found on them or in the carpet bag which they carried with them on the coach? The locked drawer of the dressing-table, which the manager had to open for him, contained only their travellers' checks and Mrs. Price's depilatory cream.

He ran the passports to earth in a suitcase under one of the beds. In due course they would have to be sent to the British Consulate, in accordance with the regulations for dealing with the effects of deceased foreigners. As a routine measure he looked through them. But the pages of entry stamps revealed no sinister pattern of travel to outlandish destinations, only the peregrinations of an ordinary couple who took a holiday somewhere in Europe every year.

But what was this that fell to the floor out of Mrs. Price's passport? A half-sheet of ordinary squared paper, perhaps torn out of a school exercise-book. He unfolded it and read.

12th	5.00	Primavera
13th	6.00	Baptistry
14th	12.15	Salvadori
15th	4.30	Bella Vista

This, clearly, was a list of appointments: in front of the Primavera in the Uffizi Gallery one day, in the Baptistry the next. Both these were in Florence, but the next was at the Villa Salvadori near Lucca at the very time when the kidnapping had happened. They had kept the appointment, with fatal results. And tomorrow was the fifteenth; they had another one tomorrow afternoon at the Bella Vista, wherever that was. Not that it mattered. There was no point in keeping watch to see if their date was kept by the other party, who would surely conclude from the press and television coverage that his presence would serve no useful purpose, since the Prices had been shot dead.

When Barbetti rang headquarters to report this discovery to his chief, Ciampi reacted sharply. "This is of great importance. Someone must show photographs of the Price couple to the attendants at the Uffizi and the Baptistry, in case they remember the Prices and can describe to us the person who kept the appointment with them."

It was an outside chance, unlikely to yield results but the sort of thing that had to be covered. But there was a difficulty. "We have no suitable photos, *capo*, of the Prices."

True, Ciampi thought. The police photographer's pictures showed two faces distorted in the agony of sudden death, and were far from suitable. "They will appear in the tourists' holiday photos," he said. "The laboratory people must stay late and develop them, I will arrange it now. And when you get back here we will analyze the results."

When Barbetti arrived at headquarters, Ciampi was already poring over the prints from the first few reels to have been processed by the laboratory. The results were disappointing, because the group consisted of up-market tourists who did not photograph each other in vulgar laughing groups. The figures in views of the gardens they had visited were almost always in the background. One photographer had taken shots of people sitting round lunch-tables in restaurants, but the Prices were not among them.

"It appears that they did not eat with the others," said Barbetti. "And they left the group frequently, on the excuse of sightseeing in Florence. We may be unlucky."

"And where are the Hansons?" Ciampi grumbled. "We need likenesses of them too."

Barbetti pointed with his pencil at a woman with elaborately dressed blonde hair, standing in the background of a view of a garden. "That must be the Signora Hanson; I do not remember such a golden hair-do in any of our interviews with the tourists."

"But why does she not appear in any of these?" Ciampi asked as he examined the lunch-table shots again. "Ah, here she is, but this is of no use to us."

The golden curls were in evidence. But she had a napkin up to her mouth, which hid most of her face.

"And that is probably the husband." Barbetti pointed to the man next to her. He had thinning straw-colored hair which they did not remember from the interviews, but he had turned away from the camera to talk to his other neighbor, so that only the back of his head was visible.

In a picture taken at a different lunch-table, the golden-haired lady had bent down to pick up her fallen table-napkin, and her husband had also bent down to assist. Again, they had contrived to hide their faces. "These are certainly the Hansons," said Ciampi. "And they seem to dislike being photographed, but why?"

One of the last reels to come from the laboratory yielded a view of the Garzoni garden, with the Prices in the foreground looking straight at the camera. This was what Ciampi was hoping for. He sent the negative back to the laboratory with a request for an enlargement of the two heads, and asked for a dozen copies. There would be a heavy demand for them from the press.

Barbetti was going through the prints again, looking for likenesses of the two black bully-boys who had caused such a commotion among the tourists in the hours before the kidnapping. There was only one picture of them, hiding their faces blatantly behind a guidebook. They were not just camera-shy. They did not care who knew that they were.

"She was right, the one who said that these two were making a mystification, to put us on a false track," Barbetti remarked.

"Who said that, Giorgio?"

"The little lady who does not dye her hair, and is mad. But perhaps she is only half mad."

The late-duty desk sergeant came into the office. "Excuse me, *Signor Commissario*. The media are here, they want a statement."

"Why? Tell them I have nothing new to say."

"Very well, *Signor Commissario*. There is also a telex for you from London."

Ciampi took the telex and read it. He knew now why the media wanted a statement from him. And he also knew that the little lady was not mad after all.

Farthingale Tours was assembled round the television set in the hotel lounge, watching the early evening news and listening to Paolo's running translation of the Rome newscaster's remarks.

"He say there is dramatic development in kidnap case, the terrorists have taken the wrong people . . . Now comes Mrs. Waters who is in London, and she speaks in English . . . no, they cover her with translation in Italian, and she says she is daughter of Mr. and Mrs. Hanson, and terrorists have telephoned her asking for big ransom, but she says no ransom because her parents are in Florida having holiday and are not being kidnap in Italy. Here now is Mrs. Hanson who is not our Mrs. Hanson, quite different, and she say she is in Florida and no kidnap. And now they ask her husband Mr. Hanson if perhaps it is some relative and he say no, all his family is in their houses and not visiting gardens in Italy, he has telephoned them and it is a mystery. Here now is Commissario Ciampi, who is saying also that is a mystery, and that is finish because now comes political commentator who says next week we have cabinet crisis.''

The commentator boomed on about the cabinet crisis, but his voice was drowned in a torrent of exclamations from Farthingale Tours. Major Gatling condemned the kidnappers as a ''ghastly shower of incompetents''. The flower-arranging lady maintained in a twee voice that nothing better could be expected of black South Africans. Nigel Monk remarked that the terrorists now had an identity problem on their hands which no psychiatrist could solve for them. Mr. Enderby-Scott assumed hopefully that the terrorists would have to let the kidnapped Hansons go, and the lugubrious woman in black made a passionate plea for the reintro-duction of the death penalty.

''Extraordinary, the whole thing!'' exclaimed Professor Winkworth, ''and quite unlike what happens in detective stories, of which I am an avid reader. In fiction the detectives are unravelling a crime which has been logically planned and coolly carried out. The criminals keep their heads, and do not make stupid mistakes in the agitation of the moment. But that is art. Life, on the contrary, is chaotic. The un-fortunate Commissario Ciampi has to unravel the thought-processes of a bunch of incompetents who kidnap the wrong people and shoot two innocent bystanders in the panic of the moment.''

Mrs. Armstrong tried to say yet again that the Prices were not innocent bystanders, but the Professor swept on. ''The tragicomedy would have more point if the people kidnapped in error proved to be as poor as church mice, so that the kidnappers had to release them. Unfortunately they seem to be quite rich enough to be acceptable substitutes.''

Tired of listening to nonsense based on a false premise,

Celia escaped to her bedroom and applied herself yet again to the telephone. Unless Commissario Ciampi was much stupider than he seemed, he would be frantic to get in touch with her as soon as he heard the news from London. She would cut a much more imposing figure if she could confront him armed with the Hansons' real name. The holiday weekend was almost over, surely someone would be at home by now to tell her. She tried the Claytons first. To her relief, they were back and Rhona answered.

"Listen, Rhona. You remember those actors you put up during the festival last year?" Celia asked. "The couple with the Down's syndrome child? You don't happen to remember their name?"

"I'm sorry, no. Why?"

"It's too complicated to explain, but it's rather important. You didn't keep the programme, by any chance?"

" 'Fraid not."

"You don't make people sign a visitors' book?"

"Oh. Sorry, yes, I didn't think of that. It's in the hall. Hold on and I'll look." After a pause, Rhona came back on the line. "Here we are. James and Paula Vincent."

"Any address?"

"Only care of their agent."

The agent was Elaine Bundry, with an address in Bloomsbury. Celia made a note of it.

"But aren't you in Italy, Celia? Is this one of your detective things? Oh goody, you must tell me all about it."

"I will when I get back. But I must go now, I'm expecting someone else to ring."

It was almost ten when Ciampi rang, sounding embarrassed. "This afternoon, Signora, you mentioned during your statement a matter which interests me concerning the identity of the two hostages. If you will be so good, I would like to hear more about it."

"I thought perhaps you might," said Celia lightly.

"I am at the hotel desk. I know it is late, but could you do me the kindness to come down to the *salone*?"

Celia hesitated. "I'll willingly talk to you, but not in any of the public rooms where we might be seen together by other members of the tour."

"I can arrange something with the management of the hotel, Signora. But why?"

"Because I want to stay alive, which might not happen if the wrong person saw us talking to each other."

Ciampi had to admit to himself that a sufferer from persecution mania could hardly have spoken in that calm, half-amused tone. He was not looking forward to the coming interview, he hated climbing down and admitting an error. This afternoon he had treated la Grant as a *stravagante* who had invented an absurd story of no interest to him. She would take her revenge and make him eat dirt.

But when they met in the manager's office, she did nothing of the kind. After a few pleasant words of greeting, she sat facing him across the desk and waiting for his first question.

"This afternoon, Signora, you said that you thought you saw a resemblance between the kidnapped couple and two British actors whose names you did not know."

"Yes. I'm sorry I was so vague," said Celia, oozing all the charm she could muster. "I know their names now, I managed to telephone someone in England who told me. They are James and Paula Vincent, and their agent is Elaine Bundry, whose address in London I can give you."

"Thank you. And now tell me, please, in what circumstances you met these people, and why you think they resemble Mr. and Mrs. Hanson."

Ceila told him about the horrific performance of *Hamlet*, and how she had given the Vincents a lift back to the Claytons' afterwards.

"But these events occurred a year ago, Signora. How can you be sure of the likeness after so long?"

"Two likenesses, Commissario. And look-alikes don't usually come in pairs."

"Nevertheless, it is a long time to remember."

"Everything about that evening is still vivid in my mind. The Vincents were rather awful people, but they had a handicapped child and I was sorry for them as well as repelled by them. Besides, the performance of *Hamlet* was nightmarishly bad."

"Even so, it is strange that it has remained so clear in your memory."

"My dear Commissario, if you'd had to sit through *Madam Butterfly* produced by a twenty-year-old madman and performed by punk rockers who couldn't sing, you wouldn't forget it in a hurry."

To his surprise, Ciampi found himself laughing. "The *impresario d'avanguardia* is a bad problem everywhere," he agreed, then stiffened again into formality. This tiny woman with the porcelain complexion seemed very self-confident, but he was not convinced by her story.

"You're not sure about this, are you?" said Celia, continuing to play her fish gently. "But I've thought of a way you could check, if you want to."

"Yes?"

"There's a book called *Spotlight*, a casting directory listing all the actors and actresses seeking work on the British stage. It contains photographs of all of them. If you could get hold of a copy, you could show the Vincents' pictures to other people on the tour. If they said 'yes, that's the Hansons', you'd know you were on firm ground."

Normally, Ciampi would have resented being told what to do, especially by a foreigner: and a female one, which made it worse. But the suggestion had been put forward modestly, and he decided in the end that there was no need to give himself an indigestion because he had not thought of it first. It involved knowledge of the British theatrical world that he could not be expected to possess.

"I will try to find a copy of this book," he said, making a note. "Also, I will ask our colleagues in London to make enquiries concerning the Vincents."

"Good. Shall we discuss my persecution mania now?"

The calm directness of her question startled him into an apology. "I am so sorry about our bad thoughts this afternoon."

"That's all right, I probably sounded like a lunatic. I bear you no malice."

"You are very kind, Signora. Tell me now, please, why you have this great fear of your fellow-tourists."

Celia explained about the doping of her drink and the Hansons' attempt to get into her bedroom. "They were afraid, you see, that I would expose them as impostors."

"But Signora, the Hansons are out of circulation, as you might say. You are no longer in danger from them."

Celia explained that, on the contrary, she was in danger from some unknown member of the tour who had masterminded the Hanson operation. Asked why she thought such a person existed, she told Ciampi about the Marchesa's cream jug and Mrs. Hanson's performance afterwards at the dinner-table.

Ciampi stared at her, mesmerised by her doll-like appearance. What she had just told him held together with a sort of mad logic, he had to look into it further.

"But your dinner companions were ordinary tourists," he said, "with no background suggestion of international crime."

"That's what it looked like, but appearance can be deceptive." She went through her list of suspects for him, giving her reasons for and against each. "If you like, I can try to find out more about these people in casual conversation."

Her manner offended him. She was behaving as if they were two colleagues consulting over a case, and his defences went up at once. But they came down again quickly. After all, she was only offering to act as an ordinary police informer, why should he resent that?

"Do please chat them up, so to speak," he said. "And please listen particularly for any information concerning the

100

past of Mr. and Mrs. Price, who appear to be key figures in this affair.''

"Yes, where do they fit in? It's very puzzling. Why did they have to be killed, when the armed gardeners were allowed to stay alive?"

Ciampi seethed with suppressed rage. How dare she trespass on his province? "These are questions which my colleagues and I are considering," he said and stood up to end the interview.

Celia went back to her room, reasonably satisfied with her performance. Knowing the Hansons' real name had given her the confidence that she had lacked before. She knew she had not convinced him, he would go on dithering until the photos of the Vincents from *Spotlight* had been identified as the Hansons by someone else on the tour. But he had taken her seriously, and that was something.

"Technically, we are in the presence of death," said Professor Winkworth over breakfast next morning. "But we hardly knew Mr. and Mrs. Price, and I don't think we should let their demise oppress us unduly. Their relatives are being sought, and if and when they decide to join us here and take charge of the remains, a certain degree of woe on our part will of course be appropriate. Meanwhile, I see no reason why we shouldn't continue with the program of the tour."

The first stop of the day was at the Villa Medicea della Petraia, in a down-at-heel suburb of Florence. Its garden was a severe disappointment, despite the fact that its layout had remained unchanged since it was made in the sixteenth century. It consisted largely of narrow terraces on a steep south-facing slope, planted out with scruffy daisies and French marigolds, with a few unhappy-looking lemon and hibiscus bushes in pots as light relief. "This is what happens, unfortunately," said the Professor, "when a historic garden falls into the hands of a municipal parks department."

Celia had carefully not mentioned to Ciampi that the work of chatting up the suspects was to be shared between herself and a seventeen-year-old girl, in case he thought it unserious and off-putting. But she and Jane had worked out a division of conversational labor, and as Farthingale Tours toiled up the steep slope of the garden under a broiling sun, Jane chatted up the dreadful George, while Celia attached herself to Lady Carstairs.

"How nice for you that your stepson's able to come on holiday with you," she said.

This proved a popular theme. Lady Carstairs smiled dotingly through her heavy make-up. "Such a dear boy. He is impatient with life's little conventions and I think some members of our party look down their snuffly, bourgeois noses at him because of that. But underneath he is a true gentleman, a real knight-errant with a heart of gold. I would be lost without him."

Celia decided that George's grip on the old lady, and probably also on her money, must be even stronger than she had imagined. "He lives near you then?" she asked.

"More than that, we've set up house together. But tell me about yourself, my dear. You're still very pretty, why have you no man to look after you?"

In the interest of research, Celia took this lying down. "Not everyone's as lucky as you are. Is George on holiday from his job?"

She hesitated. "In a way, yes. But I worry about you, my dear, a woman deteriorates without a man to look after. If you neglect your opportunities it will soon be too late. I wouldn't touch Major Gatling with a bargepole, he rings false somehow, but what about Mr. Monk?"

Celia said firmly that she was not interested in either of them, and tried to steer the conversation back to George. But the wily old lady went on counter-attacking with expressions of concern for Celia's sexual prosperity, and prevented any further mention of George as they toiled on up the sun-baked slope of the dispiriting public garden.

Well ahead of them George himself was striding up the hill, with Jane trotting along beside him in an attitude of admiration.

"The ol' dear's OK," he told her. "Don't you be put off by wot she does to 'er face. She's blind as a bat, pore thing, 'as to pile it on thick before it registers in the lookin' glass. Every so often I tell 'er she looks like a cherry meringue gateau an' she cools it a bit, but that never lasts long."

"It's very nice of you to come and keep her company on this trip," said Jane.

He looked at her sharply. "She's keepin' me company, more like. Comin' on this jaunt was my idea. Wanted to get away from me business for a week, and took 'er along."

"You're a businessman, then?" Jane asked admiringly.

" 'Straight." He threw her a look, as if defying her to disbelieve him. "I'm in earth-movin' equipment."

They were half-way up the slope, and the sun was beating down mercilessly. "George, I want you," called Lady Carstairs from behind them.

He trotted back obediently.

"Be angelic, dear boy, and find out if there's anything worth seeing at the top of this dreadful hill. If not, I shan't go up."

Word was passed back to her through the Farthingale Tours grapevine that, according to the Professor, there was an exquisite Renaissance fountain on the top terrace.

"Very well then, dear boy, I'll try to make it, but I shall need your arm."

The rearrangement which resulted made it possible for Celia and Jane to compare notes.

"Let's take the obvious solution first," said Celia. "George is lying. He says he's in earth-moving equipment because it's true, he drives a digger for a construction company. He says he's in business to convince us that he can pay his way, and isn't a rent boy on the make. It was a bit over the top to imply that he was paying for the old lady too, but a man in his humiliating position would be tempted to overdo it."

"I agree, Celia, that's the obvious solution. What's the other one?"

"What worries me is, why did they come on this trip? They'd have avoided a lot of embarrassment if they'd rented a holiday love-nest somewhere and got their urges out of their systems there. Instead they decided to have a whole coachload of people pointing the finger at them and thinking there's only one reason why a fat cat on her last legs should go off on holiday with a lusty yobbo in tow. Why?"

"You mean, it's not a sex thing. They had to come, and risk being embarrassed, because they were masterminding the Hansons?"

"It's possible. This whole affair's so fantastic that one can't rule anything out."

Farthingale Tours had reached the top terrace of the garden. But the fountain which was to have gladdened their eyes was nowhere to be seen.

"How extraordinary, it should be here," said the Professor. "A very elaborate fountain by no less a sculptor than Niccolo Tribolo."

A park attendant, asked where it was, said that it was "*in restauro*", and would be back in position when the restoration had been completed.

"It is a very suggestive fountain," said Paolo.

"To avoid any misunderstanding," said the Professor, "I should explain that '*suggestivo*' in Italian means 'charming' or 'beautiful'. You've seen it, have you, Paolo?"

"Many times, *Signor Professore*. On top of it is a bronze woman by Giovanni di Bologna; some say she is city of Florence, but I think more likely she is the Venus. She was not always here, for many years she was in the garden of the Villa Castello lower down the hill . . ." He went on to describe the fountain in enthusiastic detail.

"Thank you, Paolo," said Professor Winkworth when

he had finished. "That was almost as good as seeing it for ourselves."

Such an intimate knowledge of Renaissance sculpture seemed to Celia extraordinary in a young man standing in as a substitute courier for a travel agency. "You're obviously fond of beautiful things, Paolo. How do you come to know so much about them?"

"Some day perhaps I tell you," he said with a smile, then moved on to catch up with the Professor.

❦ SIX ❦

That morning Ciampi had arrived early at headquarters and collected various overnight messages. The helicopter used by the kidnappers had been found abandoned. According to London, the Hansons had booked with Farthingale Tours from a service flat they had rented in an expensive West End block, and occupied only at intervals. They had left no clue to their permanent address. The explosives experts had examined the door of the Greek Temple which the kidnappers had blown open, and reached interesting conclusions which he must think about later, because he was due to report now to Judge Merlini, the *giudice istruttore* or examining magistrate who was technically in charge of the case.

He loathed Merlini, and Merlini loathed him. They were both prima donnas, but as Merlini was Ciampi's superior, he had the whip-hand.

"Fanciful," said Merlini when Ciampi mentioned the possibility that the two supposed hostages were a pair of actors, and that the kidnapping was a put-up job. If Ciampi had produced a more humdrum theory, Merlini would have called him unimaginative.

"I have sent a man to Rome," said Ciampi, "to find us a copy of this British theatrical directory."

"Why Rome? Why did you not ask London to send you one?"

"That would take time. This theory must be tested quickly, so that we know whether we are dealing with a real kidnap situation, or with a mystification. The film companies using the Cinecittà Studios often use English actors, one of them will lend us a copy."

"Who did you send?"

"Ruggero."

"It was a waste of skilled manpower to send a man like that on such an errand."

"This is not a matter on which you are required to express an opinion," said Ciampi with an acid smile. The magistrature had no operational control over the police; who he sent was no concern of Merlini's.

In due course Ciampi escaped into his car, and was soon showing his official pass at the entrance gate to the technical area of Pisa airport. He drove on round the perimeter road, and found that *Elicotteri Toscani* did business from a small hangar beyond the Alitalia ones. It contained two small three-seater machines. But for obvious reasons its big Sikorsky, the main workhorse of the firm's fleet, was absent. Just before dusk the previous day it had been located from the air, standing abandoned in a lonely alpine meadow in the Orecchiella nature reserve, sixty kilometres to the north in the hills of the Garfagnana.

Ciampi walked into the glassed-in enclosure in one corner which served as an office. It was occupied by an exhausted-looking blonde secretary bowed over her machine and a middle-aged man with the taut, tidy look of an ex-soldier.

Ciampi flashed his official card and introduced himself. "Signor Donegani? You know that your helicopter has been found?"

"Yes. When can I have it back?"

"We will discuss that presently. Meanwhile, I would like

to interview your pilot, who I think had a disagreeable experience.''

"It was I who had the experience, Commissario, and it was indeed disagreeable. I always pilot the Sikorsky myself.''

"Please tell me, then, about this whole affair from the beginning. Who hired the helicopter?''

"The reservation was made in the name of a firm of shoe manufacturers called Neri, who have a factory near Lucca.''

"When?''

"A week ago. It was for a very normal assignment, for us almost routine. I was to pick up a group of foreign buyers at the factory and transport them to a restaurant in the mountains, where they were to lunch. After the lunch, I was to bring them here in time to catch late afternoon flights to Paris and Amsterdam.''

"The reservation was by telephone or in writing?''

"Both. They phoned last week, and I asked for a written confirmation.'' He rummaged in a file. "Here it is.''

Ciampi took the single sheet of paper. It bore the letterhead of one of the shoe manufacturing firms which abounded in the heavily populated plain between Lucca and the foothills of the Apuan Alps. In addition to confirming the details of the booking, it gave a sketch-map showing the location of the factory, and also of the area of waste ground behind it where the helicopter could land.

"And the phone call, who took it?'' Ciampi asked.

"Maria here.''

Ciampi switched his questions to the secretary. "Man or woman?''

"I'm sorry. I don't remember.''

"Italian or foreign?''

She pondered. "I'm sorry.''

"But you would have thought it odd if a foreigner was making a booking on behalf of a local firm.''

"Perhaps, but I don't remember.''

Giving her up as hopeless, Ciampi made Donegani tell

the story of his "unpleasant experience" with the kidnappers.

"I landed on the waste ground as arranged, and went to the factory, but the place seemed deserted, local people told me later that the firm had gone out of business months ago. A side door was open so I went in to see if I could find anyone. What I found was three masked men with guns who tied me up and gagged me."

"Tell me what they were like. Any clue to their nationality?"

"They spoke English, but with an American accent."

"Were they white or black?"

"How could I tell? They wore hoods."

"But did you notice what colour their hands were?"

Donegani laughed grimly. "One notices very little with one's head in a sack."

"And then the three of them took off in your helicopter?"

"That's right, I'd even left the motor running for them."

Neat, Ciampi thought. If the kidnappers removed their hoods before they left the building, anyone who happened to be watching would probably fail to notice the change of pilot. Even if he did, it would not strike him as sinister.

"This machine, the controls are fairly simple?" he asked. "Anyone who knew how to pilot a helicopter could manage it?"

"No, you'd have to have a course of familiarization with Sikorskys, but there are thousands of them in operation all over the world, there would be no problem. And of course, the terrorists knew that for a party of six I would be obliged to come in the Sikorsky."

He had stayed trussed up in the deserted factory till the police came to rescue him late in the afternoon, having been tipped off by an anonymous telephone call to police headquarters in Lucca.

There was a map on the office wall, and he made Donegani show him where the shoe factory was.

"Here, Commissario."

"And the restaurant?"

"Here. The Cigogna at Castiglione di Garfagnana."

Ciampi knew it. A favorite choice for business lunches and enormous family feasts on Sundays. The kidnappers had been clever over this too. The Villa Salvadori was almost on a straight line between the factory and the restaurant, and its real destination in the nature reserve was only a few kilometres on in the same direction. In other words, the kidnappers had adhered to the flight path which Donegani would have registered in advance with the control tower at Pisa. Apart from making an unscheduled stop at the Villa Salvadori *en route*, they had done nothing to alert the authorities that anything illegal was taking place. By the time the helicopter's markings had been established and passed on to the air force at Pisa, it would have reached the nature reserve ten minutes' flying time away, and kidnappers and victims would be speeding off in the car which had no doubt been waiting at the rendezvous.

"What worries me is, when can I have my helicopter back?" Donegani was asking. "I need it for a booking tomorrow."

"I'm not sure. You can ring the *questura* in Castelnuovo di Garfagnana this afternoon and ask them. The fingerprint people and so on are up in Orecchiella already, and I am going there now."

To avoid hours of delay on winding mountain roads, he had himself flown there in a police helicopter. The kidnappers had planned cleverly yet again in choosing this lonely area to abandon the hijacked Sikorsky and transfer to a road vehicle. On a weekday early in the season there would be few people about in its vast spaces, and any who were would assume that the machine was there on legitimate nature-reserve business. Once in the getaway vehicle, the kidnappers had a bewildering choice of roads open to them, leading out of the park in all directions. The Leghorn-Genoa *autostrada* was within striking distance. But it was far more likely that they were using a local hideout. There was no lack of holiday homes and skiing chalets for hire in the surrounding valleys and Ciampi foresaw a tedious round of enquiries in the estate agencies of Lucca and Castelnuovo.

The police pilot spotted the Sikorsky in an alpine meadow screened from the rough track across the hillside by a belt of trees, and landed at a respectful distance from it. The photographers and fingerprint people who had driven up by road from Castelnuovo were already there.

The inspector in charge had little of interest to report. "The fingerprints are not hopeful. Whoever was at the controls wore gloves."

"And they left nothing behind?"

A scarf was produced, and a half-eaten bar of chocolate. But it had been broken not bitten, and there were no helpful tooth marks. In any case, it and the scarf probably belonged to the Sikorsky's rightful owner. The only other possible clue was a fragment of material with a few small feathers attached to it, which had caught on a projection beside the door. "From a quilt, or something similar," Ciampi decided. "What did they want with that?"

"They drove the getaway vehicle right up to the helicopter," said the inspector from Castelnuovo, pointing out some wheeltracks in the grass.

"Understandable," Ciampi commented. "If the female hostage was still reacting hysterically to her capture, they would want to get her into it as quickly and unobtrusively as possible."

But had Mrs. Hanson reacted hysterically, or had she been putting on an act? Had the pair of them been paid for their performance, then dropped by the kidnappers at some convenient point, to make their way quietly back to England? Ciampi wished he knew.

Presently he was called to the telephone in the police car which had come up from Castelnuovo. Barbetti at headquarters in Pisa wanted him.

"*Ciao, capo.* I have news for you. Judge Merlini feels

that he should see the hijacked helicopter for himself, and asks you to remain at the scene till he arrives.''

Barbetti had tried to keep his voice neutral for the sake of anyone who might be listening on the circuit, but Ciampi could detect the undertone of suppressed rage. Merlini would be travelling by road, he was afraid of air travel, so Ciampi would have to hang about for an hour and a half at least with nothing to do, waiting for him to arrive. He would probably bring a press photographer with him, and a shot of him standing beside the hijacked helicopter, detecting nothing in particular, would appear in the evening papers.

''And you have made the arrangements for this afternoon, Giorgio?''

''At the Uffizi and the Baptistry? Yes, *capo*, the pictures of Mr. and Mrs. Price were sent to the *questura* in Florence an hour ago.''

''Good. And the appointment which they made for this afternoon at the Villa Bella Vista must also be covered. It is an outside chance, but in a case like this one must not neglect anything.''

Such an outside chance, Barbetti decided, that it was a waste of time to follow it up. But with the chief in his present mood there was no point in protesting.

''What progress with the casting directory for la Grant?'' Ciampi asked.

''Nothing yet. Ruggero is doing his best.''

''Ring him again. Tell him to hurry.''

Barbetti decided he would do no such thing. He admired Ciampi, and was willing to bear the brunt of his nervous tensions. But he was not prepared to needle other people unnecessarily on his chief's behalf and give them the impression that Ciampi was a neurotic fusspot.

Mrs. Waters had left her answering machine switched on all morning. On investigating at lunch-time she was surprised and displeased to find that the kidnapper had left another message on it, a furious one, ordering her to turn off the machine and answer him in person. She ignored it, but when it was repeated in even fouler language an hour later, she decided to alert Inspector Tomlinson.

"This is absurd," he said. "Surely they must know by now that they've got the wrong hostages?"

He came round at once and made her turn off the machine. In her present tetchy mood she was clearly incapable of chatting up the kidnapper and keeping him on the line while the technicians tried to trace the call, so he decided to take it himself.

It came shortly after two. "Hullo Miz Waters, you decided to talk to us at last?"

"Hello there," said Tomlinson. "How are you feeling this afternoon?"

A pause. "Who the hell's that?"

"Mrs. Waters asked me to talk to you in her place."

"Did she now? Who the hell are you?"

"Inspector Tomlinson. Scotland Yard."

This produced a furious outburst from the other end, to the effect that Mrs. Waters was a prisoner of the police, who were preventing her from paying the ransom. Tomlinson tried hard to get across the message that the wrong hostages had been taken, but it was like talking to a brick wall.

"Surely you've seen the TV news or read the papers? Mr. and Mrs. Hanson are in Bermuda, they say you've made a mistake, their daughter says you've made a mistake. Everyone's agreed that you've got the wrong couple."

"We seen the television, we seen two white people what say they's Mr. and Mrs. Hanson, how do we know it's true? You people control the media, you can say what you like."

"Haven't the hostages told you you've made a mistake?"

"They says that, but they got their passports with them. Edward and Ethel Hanson, it says on them. She got a big diamond on her finger, they got expensive clothes. They's lying, you's all lying. You tell Mrs. Waters she better get that ransom goin'. We give her a week to fix it, then we start cutting off fingers and ears. 'Bye now.''

Again the electronic equipment gave the call a continental origin, but could not trace it beyond the international exchange.

After lunch and the usual wanderings caused by the Professor's insecure grasp of geography, Farthingale Tours was visiting the garden of the Villa Capponi, on the other side of Florence from the dispiriting Villa Medicea della Petraia. It was a jewel, beautifully laid out in the sixteenth century and beautifully kept by its private owners, but small enough to be manageable. Celia had fallen in love with it at once.

Mr. and Mrs. Enderby-Scott were standing on a terraced lawn overlooking a superb view of the city. Celia joined them, and they exchanged generalities about the view and the beauties of the garden.

Having, as she thought, softened them up sufficiently, Celia began her inquisition. ''You live in London, don't you? That doesn't give much scope for gardening as a rule.''

''Not as a rule, no.''

''Though it's wonderful what people manage to do with tiny backyards in Kensington and Chelsea.''

This produced no reply.

''You knew a lot about the old roses, I remember. Are you frustrated gardeners, longing to escape from London?''

''Not really, no.'' Mr. Enderby-Scott turned to his wife. ''There's a nice-looking parterre over there, through the gate with the stone griffins on. Shall we go and look at it?''

Left alone on the terrace, Celia gave them no marks for sociable behavior and a high place on her list of suspects.

The Professor, accompanied by the owner of the garden, was leading Farthingale Tours down from the terrace into the Villa Capponi's secret garden. It was much smaller than the one from which the Hansons had been kidnapped at the Villa Salvadori and earlier in date, a charming open-air room with a window in the wall which overlooked the view.

"This secret garden was laid out by Gino Capponi himself, soon after he bought the property in 1572," said the Professor. " Originally there was an underground access to it from the house, like the one at the Villa Salvadori, for use in windy weather. But it was blocked up some time in the eighteenth century. And I'd like to tell you while we are here of a curious discovery that I made last night. I thought I'd look up the authorities on the Villa Salvadori, and do you know, the underground passage from its *giardino segreto* to the Villa must have been blocked at some time in the past, and reopened in modern times. Georgina Masson doesn't mention the passage at all, and I imagine she would have done if it had been open when she published her book in 1961. But I also looked into a guidebook to these gardens published by a Mrs. Aubrey le Blond in 1912. She tells one to take the electric tram from outside the Hotel Universo in Lucca, and walk two miles from the point where the tram puts you down and then up that long cypress avenue to the villa . . . How dogged tourists were in those days, and how much healthier we would be if we had not succumbed to the internal combustion engine, but of course they would have taken a month to see what we're seeing in a week . . ."

Part of his audience was getting restive and beginning to drift away, and he noticed this. "To cut a long story short," he went on, "the good lady was rather sniffy about the Villa Salvadori and especially about the secret garden, which she dismissed as 'curious rather than beautiful'. One of the curious features that struck her was a blocked-up doorway half-way down one side, which had been turned rather clumsily into a sort of alcove. She was told that it marked the entrance to a passage which had formerly existed, leading into the basement of the house. That seems to me conclusive, and in view of our distressing experiences there yesterday I thought it would interest you."

Nigel Monk was standing next to Celia. Remembering that she was supposed to be finding out more about his background, she turned to him with a half-smile which invited conversation.

He turned towards her, full of concern. "Ah, my dear Celia. So you have decided to come in from the cold."

"I'm not sure what you mean."

"I was watching you after the kidnapping yesterday. They were all talking about it, but you went very quiet and said nothing. Did it frighten you very much?"

There was a glint of mockery behind the rimless glasses as he embarked on a repeat of his silly psychiatric joke. Celia decided to play along with it. "The whole thing's too awful to think about," she said, affecting a delicate shudder.

He shook his head sadly. "In other words you've erected a mental block about it, on a completely conscious level. Oh, Celia, that's not wise."

"I think the way they all dwell on it is rather morbid."

"Tell me about yourself, Celia. I can probably help more if I know a little about your background. Do you have a job?"

"Yes."

"What sort of a job?"

"I don't think I want to tell you."

"My dear girl, you're heading for disaster. No one can help you if you shut your friends out."

"Tell me about your job first."

He looked deeply into her eyes. "Celia, don't start being too interested in me. That would only lead to heartbreak."

She gazed solemnly into his face, then burst into wild laughter. "You pompous buffoon, come off it."

He put on an affronted expression. "I don't know what you mean."

"Oh yes you damn well do."

"Celia, you are beyond help," he said despairingly and turned away. But he was having trouble keeping a straight face.

It was four o'clock and time to pass on to the Villa Bella Vista, whose owner had been educated at Eton and Oxford.

116

Having become more English than the English, he had swept away his geometrical parterres and replaced them with a tangle of higgledy-piggledy mixed borders and secluded nooks in the English style. In one such nook, under a rustic arbor which would have been more in place outside a thatched cottage in Wiltshire, Jane Armstrong found herself face to face with Major Gatling, and said "good afternoon".

Inflamed by this rash remark, the Major decided to exert his fascination. What, he asked, was a pretty girl like Jane doing on an older-generation tour like this, instead of having it off happily with her boyfriend at home? No boyfriend? Perhaps she preferred older men. No? That was a mistake if he might say so. Boys her age were brutal and clumsy. Far better to start with someone experienced, who knew what he was doing.

Jane retorted that she had no intention of "starting" with anyone.

"Why not?" he insisted. "You'll have to, some time."

"No I won't, if I don't want to. Queen Elizabeth the first managed all her life without."

"Didn't know what she was missing, silly woman. Nor do you."

Jane said that although the Virgin Queen might have had her faults, no serious student of her achievements could regard her as silly. When she tried to dodge past him, he side-stepped to block her escape.

"Please let me go," she said, "or I shall have to make a scene."

"Hullo, Jane," said Celia, appearing round the corner of a hedge. Seeing her dismayed face, she added: "Is anything wrong?"

"No, nothing," said Major Gatling, cool and composed. "We were just admiring this little white tea-rose."

Celia studied the rose, which was trained over the arbor. "You've not seen it before?"

"No. Too tender for English gardens, I imagine. Charming, though."

Celia choked back an impulse to point out that the rose was an Alberic Barbier, grown in gardens all over England, and a wichuraiana, not a tea. What was a man who did not know this doing on a horticultural tour?

"Are you a keen gardener?" she asked.

"Alas, no."

"How surprising. Yet you came with us visiting gardens?"

"Yes, but I'm interested in the garden sculpture rather than the vegetation, in fact I deal in these things at home. Just as a hobby, but I needed something to keep me amused when I came out of the army."

"What a fascinating hobby," said Celia.

"Yes, I started it up in my garden in a small way, and it's become quite a paying proposition. There's a huge demand for good eighteenth-century pieces when one can get hold of them, and I try to rescue architectural details like doorframes and balustrading when a house is being demolished. I've got a chap just started up in the stables who makes reproduction urns and so on."

"But I've been looking for a centre-piece for my rose garden for years!" Celia lied. "I'd love to see your collection."

"Good. When we get back to the hotel I'll give you my business card."

Later, when they had shaken him off, Celia said: "Oh, my poor Jane, was he very nasty?"

"Weird more than anything, he was like a sex-starved weasel hungering for prey. I bet his sculpture's kinky."

"I suspect that it's imaginary."

"Oh, Celia. You mean, the business doesn't exist?"

"It's possible. Suppose he's the Hansons' minder. A professional interest in garden sculpture would explain what a man with no horticultural knowledge was doing on this tour. And if he has some sort of secret service background—"

"That's right. He has. Dad says he's spooky."

"Then there we are. Oh dear, how I hate having to suspect all sorts of people who are probably quite innocent. Let's go and talk to someone nice for a change."

In a kind of orchard they fell in with Paolo, who proclaimed himself delighted with "this strange, untidy garden, so English".

A depressed-looking stranger to the group was talking earnestly to the owner of the garden. "Who's that man with the Barone?" Celia asked.

"It is a secret, nevertheless I tell you," said Paolo. "He is a policeman in his civil clothes."

"Oh, not more questions, surely?" complained one of the women from Cheshire.

"I think no, he talks with the Professor and the Barone, no one else."

"What about?" Celia asked.

"Only the flies on the wall are knowing that."

Unwilling to be put off so easily, Celia questioned the Professor.

"It appears that Mrs. Armstrong was right about the Prices," he explained. "According to the police they have a sinister background after all. Far from wandering down to the lake out of sheer cussedness, they met the helicopter by appointment."

Celia asked how the police knew this, and he told her about the list of appointments they had found in the Prices' bedroom.

"But this doesn't make sense," she protested. " If they were keeping an appointment, why did the people in the helicopter shoot them?"

"That is one of the questions which makes real life more chaotic than detective fiction."

Agente Bianchi took leave of the Barone and wondered what to do next. His instructions were to mingle unobtrusively, but how did one mingle with a group of people who knew each other and noticed the presence of a stranger at once?

Failing to find a better solution, he mingled with the tour's driver, who was standing by his coach outside the gate, and lit a cigarette.

He had spent an unprofitable afternoon so far. The *Squadra Mobile* in Pisa in its wisdom had detailed him to push photographs of the Prices under the noses of the attendants in the Baptistry and in front of the Primavera in the Uffizi, where they were supposed to have had assignations. But thousands of tourists every hour poured through both places, and it was ludicrous to expect the attendants not only to recognize the murdered couple from their photographs, but also remember who had kept the appointment with them. Having drawn the expected blank at both places, the unfortunate Bianchi had been detailed to present himself at the Villa Bella Vista, which the Prices would have been visiting with their fellow-tourists if they had still been alive. He was to keep a sharp lookout for any persons unknown who might have come there hoping to transact mysterious business with the Prices, having unaccountably failed to take note of lead stories in the press and on television to the effect that they were dead.

Someone had to go through the motions of making these idiotic enquiries to protect the *Squadra Mobile* from high-level accusations of failure to be thorough. The jobs always got farmed out to the local rank and file, because all concerned knew there would be no end result.

While Bianchi chatted with the coach driver and nursed his grievance, Farthingale Tours was invited to have a look at the interior of the villa. Paolo lingered behind in the grand saloon after the main body had gone on into the next room, and Jane Armstrong, noticing this, stayed behind too.

He smiled when he saw her. "I was looking at the porcelains in this *vetrina.*"

The glass-fronted cabinet contained a small collection of greyish china with decoration in blue.

"Tell me about it, Paolo," said Jane.

"It is from the Doccia factory, established by the Marchese Carlo Ginori, about seventeen hundred forty-five, very rare. The stencil pattern on the coffee-pot is typical.''

"How come that you know so much about these old things, Paolo?"

After a short silence Paolo said: "About this I cover myself in mystery."

"Oh, not fair. You can't say there's a mystery and not tell.''

"You are too young to be told things that are sad."

"Now you've made it even worse. You're making a bid for sympathy without telling me what I'm to be sympathetic about. Besides, nobody's 'too young' nowadays, we have to take horrors in our stride before we're ten, so come along, tell me."

"When I am not being courier, I am buying very cheap if I can beautiful old things, not for myself but for my *padrone*, who sells them in his shop very expensive."

"Oh yes, that is sad," said Jane. "But how did you come to know so much about antiques?"

"That is even more sad."

"Tell me. Come on, Paolo."

After a lot more pressure, he told her the story. "You see, in my family's house were many beautiful things which our ancestors had bought since they built it in *cinquecento*, what you call sixteenth century. Now all are gone."

"Goodness, why? Where is this house?"

"It was in Fiesole. Not any more, it is burned down."

"How awful. How did that happen?"

"It happened."

"No, come on. Tell me, or I shall suspect that you set fire to it yourself."

"No, it was my mother. My father, you see, had a mistress, which is normal. This did not please my mother, but she had to accept. But what was not normal was that my father gave to this mistress, who asked him always for presents, a set of jewels which was given to my ancestor by Grand Duke Cosimo II. This my mother could not accept, so she went to live in our apartment in Rome. Then my father made his mistress to come and live with him in our family home at Fiesole, and this also my mother could not accept. So she was very angry and came one day to Fiesole and burned completely down the house.''

''With all your ancestors' things in it?''

''Everything.''

''That's dreadful. Poor Paolo.''

''It was more dreadful that there was no insurance. Moreover this mistress asked always for more money, and finally there was none. You ask me why I know about the antiquities, and I tell you. It is because there were in our house at Fiesole many antiquities which I learned about because one day they would be mine to take care of. And when there was no money and I could not go to the university, I took the only profession I know.''

''Oh, Paolo, that is sad. Do you hate it?''

''Yes. Shall we now continue the visit to this beautiful house?''

After dinner that night, Celia was summoned to the manager's office for another session with Ciampi.

''The casting directory, Signora,'' he said, gesturing languidly at the four enormous volumes of *Spotlight* which lay on the desk in front of him.

''Good gracious!'' Celia exclaimed, thanking her lucky stars that she did not have to search through them without a name to guide her. The first two volumes were devoted to men, divided into categories: leading actors, character actors, young character actors, and so on, and each category was presented in alphabetical order. The second volume contained the latter half of the alphabet, and she searched among the character actors (surely that must be the right category?) for James Vincent. He was not there. Panic seized her. Was she about to look a fool yet again in front of this tense but intelligent policeman?

Where else in the book could he be? Not in any of the

younger categories. Could lack-lustre middle-aged Jimmy have had the neck to describe himself as a leading actor, and would the editor have allowed him to get away with it? Yes, apparently. There he was, in a not very recent photo. Eyes: hazel. Height: five feet ten inches. Nothing about parts he had played, only the name of his agent, Elaine Bundry, 23 Bishop's Court, Bloomsbury.

Relieved, she showed the picture to Ciampi. "It's a bit flattering, most publicity pictures are, but quite recognizable. Now let's look for his wife."

The third and fourth volumes were devoted to actresses, but to Celia's dismay there was no cross-referencing between husbands and wives, even the fact that Joan Plowright was Lady Olivier in private life went unrecorded. Mrs. Vincent's first name was Paula but what was her stage surname? Assuming that she was far too arrogant to appear in an inferior category while her Jimmy was parading himself as a leading man, Celia looked for her among the leading actresses. Paula Martin, a younger, flatteringly lit version of Mrs. Hanson, shared an agent with James Vincent, and their photos were credited to the same photographer.

"Who will you get to identify these pictures?" she asked Ciampi.

"It will be sufficient, I think, if they are seen by Professor Winkworth."

"And will you ask him to keep quiet about them?"

"Of course."

"Thank you for pandering to my persecution mania."

The remark puzzled Ciampi for a moment. Then he remembered her theory that an agent of the kidnappers was still watching developments disguised as a member of the tour. He did not believe this, and had quite a different motive for not allowing the identification of the Hansons with the Vincents to become public knowledge. It would give him a tactical advantage if the kidnappers did not learn via the media how much the police knew.

But was it really persecution mania? Perhaps she was

right, there were so many strange aspects of this case already that one more hardly mattered. Suddenly all his tensions burst out of him.

"It is I who am feeling persecuted and full of fantasies. That terrorists should pick the wrong victim is strange enough. That they should fake a kidnapping with victims who are, as you might say, stooges, this is extraordinary beyond belief." He hit himself several times on the forehead. "Why? Why? I ask myself. A publicity stunt on behalf of the Black Power? No, one must reject that conclusion."

"There are a great many questions that baffle me completely," said Celia. "Why, for instance, was it necessary to put the gardeners in the Greek Temple? Why did the Prices, who were unarmed, have to be killed although it was all right for the gardeners to survive? And why did the Price family have an appointment with the men from the helicopter? That doesn't make sense at all. They can't have been the ground staff of the kidnap organization. If they were, the kidnappers wouldn't have shot them. If they were hostile to the kidnappers and went to meet them expecting trouble, why did they go unarmed? This is ridiculous, there must be another answer, let me think . . ."

She shut her eyes and concentrated. Ciampi was horrified at himself. His outburst had been intended as an appeal for sympathy, not an invitation to collaborate. What did she think she was doing, breaking into the police monopoly and busying herself with what did not concern her? He must put her in her place as soon as possible.

Presently she surfaced again from her thoughts. "I believe I've got it, how does this strike you? Suppose the Prices are just what they seem to be, and unconnected with this case. They slip away from the rest of the party because they're contrary people who do that sort of thing. They go down to the lake to take photos. Everyone shouts at them and they begin to come back. The helicopter lands. The kidnappers decide that they're in the way and shoot them."

Ciampi grasped at the opportunity to shoot her down.

"Signora, it is unwise to build theories without knowing the relevant facts. The Prices were there to keep an appointment, a paper to this effect was found in their room."

"I did know about that, Professor Winkworth told me, and I was just coming to it. Don't forget that our suspect is still around, the person who joined the tour to keep the Hansons, or rather the Vincents, on the rails. He's done his job, the false kidnapping's gone off according to plan with only one slight hitch: the Prices appeared on the scene at the wrong moment and had to be dealt with. There's no reason why the suspect shouldn't make himself useful by scattering a little misleading information about the place, to give you and your colleagues something irrelevant to puzzle over."

"You are saying that your suspect planted on us, so to speak, this paper with the appointments?"

"Why not? Did you compare the writing with the Prices'?"

"Of course. There is no resemblance, but that proves nothing. A third party could have provided them with a list of genuine appointments. We have no proof that your suspect exists. Moreover, how does he enter the Prices' hotel room?"

"That wouldn't be too difficult. We get back to the hotel, people are clamoring for their keys to go and tidy up before lunch. You ask for the Prices' key instead of your own and the receptionist gives it to you. He doesn't know yet that the Prices are dead, the police haven't sealed the room or told him to take special care of the key. You put the note of the appointments in the Prices' room, drop the key back on the desk while the receptionist isn't looking and go in to lunch."

Ciampi was furious. Not with la Grant, but with himself. He should have thought of this possibility.

"Your theory does not explain why the Prices were killed," he said coldly.

"Oh dear, we're back at that," moaned Celia. "There

must be an answer, let me think. There was something very odd about the set-up at the Villa Salvadori, the way we were hustled round and all that carry-on with guard dogs and shotguns. There's something we don't know about, something that they were holding back, and . . . yes, how about this? The Salvadori set-up and the helicopter are part of the same thing, I'm not sure how, but there's a secret that the gardeners and the people in the helicopter share. Outsiders mustn't know the secret, and the Prices are innocent bystanders who happen along at a moment when they are likely to discover whatever it is that outsiders mustn't know. So they get shot, leaving us to scratch our heads about the whys and wherefores.''

Ciampi relaxed a little. He had thought of that bit for himself, and no longer felt so threatened by this hypnotic, doll-like female. Moreover, he was a step ahead of her. A vague idea was taking shape in his head. He thought he knew what sort of secret the men in the helicopter shared with the gardeners.

❧ SEVEN ❧

The police car halted outside the formidable entrance gate of the Villa Salvadori. Ciampi's driver got out and rang the bell, setting off a furious barking inside the gate. After a longish wait the small door in it opened, to reveal Emilia holding two infuriated Alsatians by the collar.

"I have more questions to ask," Ciampi shouted over the noise that the dogs were making. Three more of them had appeared from nowhere and were snarling at him with bared yellow teeth.

"Wait while I shut up the dogs," Emilia shouted back, looking far from pleased, and shut the postern door in his face. Time passed. The barking stopped. Emilia came back and let him in.

"I will speak first to Giovanni Fabbri," Ciampi told her.

The courtyard in front of the villa was flanked on both sides by one-storey buildings. The Fabbri family lived in the range on one side, and to judge from the noise, which had started again, the Alsatians were shut up on the other.

Emilia left him abruptly at the Fabbris' door and withdrew into the villa. He knocked and found them all there: Giovanni, his wife and son and Luigi Carlini, his cousin. Seeing no point in separating them, he sat down in their kitchen and put to them the question that puzzled him: when the helicopter arrived, they were standing beside the two tourists clutching their shotguns. How had this come about?

"We had been working in the garden theatre," said Giovanni. "But it was hot and the work was hard, and we needed a little pause. So we decided to go down to the woods for some shooting, and on the way we met the two tourists, who were coming up from the lake."

"But at first you did not tell me this," Ciampi objected. "You claimed to have grabbed your guns and rushed out to meet the threat from the helicopter. Why did you not tell me the truth?"

"We were going shooting when we should have been working," said Fabbri with an impudent leer, "and we were afraid you would report us to the owners of the villa."

This was nonsense, and everyone in the room knew it. Ciampi was convinced that the gardeners had been escorting the two stragglers back to the main body of tourists under armed guard. But why? He did not know. To tax them with it would only lead to further loss of dignity.

In his brief-case he had a report from the police explosives experts. According to them, the kidnappers had not blown open the door of the Greek Temple. They had let off a small charge of gelignite against it, to disguise the fact that they had opened the padlock with a key. Where had the key come from? He put the question to them all. They became sullen and uncomfortable, but said they did not know. Who was in charge of the key? Emilia Strozzi. He had hoped that this revelation would produce a crack in their common front against him, with the three gardeners on one side of the crack and Emilia, the caretaker of the villa, on the other. But he could detect no sign of it.

Giving them up as hopeless, he went up to the villa and attacked Emilia on the subject of the key. "Come, Emilia. Who supplied the criminals with a key to that padlock if you did not?"

"Am I the good God that I should know?" she snapped.

"The Fabbris and Carlini say that the key was entrusted to you, and kept by you at the villa."

"It was kept with all the other keys in the kitchen. Anyone could have taken it and had a copy made. People come and go all the time."

"In spite of the dogs?"

"We shut them up when tradesmen deliver."

"Let us talk now about the padlock," said Ciampi, swallowing his frustration. "It was renewed quite recently, and is of good quality. Why was this done?"

"The old lock had rusted. Tools and garden materials are kept in there. It had to be kept secure."

"It seems, Emilia, that you have become obsessed with security very recently. Why? By February, when you obtained those savage dogs, everything worth stealing in the villa had already been stolen."

"But not all the thieves know that. We feared for ourselves, there might be violence when they found nothing. That was why I wrote to the Signor Marchese and asked him to let us have guard dogs."

"When my men searched the woods for clues, they found wires stretched between trees at knee height, and signs that they had been connected to an alarm system. Why was this necessary?"

"For the same reason."

"But the thefts have gone on for five years. The last one was in the autumn. Why did you wait for so long before you obtained the guard dogs?"

He put the question several times in different ways, without getting a coherent answer. Forced into a corner, she said at last. "We were afraid also of the sex murderer."

Campi knew about this in outline. A maniac was at large in the district, who preyed on courting couples. Housing conditions were cramped in the villages, and it was not uncommon for lovers to meet for heavy petting and more in hiding places out of doors. Several such couples had been knifed where they lay, in woodland or secluded corners of gardens. A sadistic voyeur was clearly responsible.

"It happened once here," said Emilia. "In the woods behind the open-air theatre."

"When was this?"

"Some time during the winter, I don't remember."

"Who was killed?"

"Andrea Vanucci. The village builder."

"And the woman?"

Emilia became very tight lipped. "We do not know. She escaped."

"So it was after this murder that you obtained the guard dogs?"

"Yes. It was for our safety. The gardeners sleep always with a loaded shotgun ready."

Campi made a mental note to learn more about this from the inspector dealing with the Vanucci case, and passed on. "When the English tourists arrived, you asked the professor in charge to keep them together, because there had been unpleasant incidents with intruders in the grounds. What were you referring to?"

Emilia hinted vaguely at sinister goings-on of one kind or another. In the end, he made her admit that the only serious one was this murder.

"Signora, we know that where sex is concerned the English are incapable of restraining themselves. But surely you did not expect that these middle-aged bourgeois would couple themselves in pairs on the grass like animals, and fall victim to a sex murderer who had entered the grounds during the short period of the visit, when the guard dogs were shut up?"

"I decided that every precaution for their safety must be taken," said Emilia sullenly.

Frustrated and tense at having found out so little, Ciampi had himself driven to the Lucca *questura*, the centre which was investigating the series of sex murders. When he questioned the inspector in charge of the case, it became clear at once that the murder of Vanucci in the grounds of the Villa Salvadori differed from others in the series. There was only one victim. In every other case both sexual partners had been killed.

"How do you account for this departure from the norm?" Ciampi asked. "Did the woman escape?"

"Possibly, but we doubt it. We have also asked ourselves if the woman had left the scene before the arrival of the maniac, but we reject that possibility."

"Oh? Why?"

"The psychology. It is clear from the other cases that the murderer is a voyeur, who kills when he sees two people engaged in sexual activity."

"Then what is your explanation?"

"The murderer recognized the woman and spared her."

Ciampi was amazed. "You really think that?"

"It is the only possibility, and we know who the woman was. Emilia Strozzi, the caretaker at the villa. We assume that the murderer must be one of her brothers or cousins, she is related to half the village."

"I am not convinced that this murder was part of the series," said Ciampi grimly.

"But the method was the same, a knife. The circumstances were the same. Vanucci had brought a rubber groundsheet and some blankets, to make everything comfortable. He was undressed except for his shirt, there was even a used *preservativo*."

"Still attached?"

"No. In proximity."

"Did you check that the contents of this *preservativo* corresponded with Vanucci's blood group?"

"No, but it is common knowledge in the village that Vanucci was Emilia Strozzi's lover."

"What is common knowledge in villages is not always true. I think it very possible that a carefully disseminated rumor provided the murdered man with a mythical sexual partner to go with the misleading *messa in scena*. When did the murder happen?''

''On the seventh of February.''

''Who makes love out of doors in February?'' Ciampi asked.

''The weather at the time was unusually warm for the time of year.''

Ciampi brushed this aside. ''I am not convinced by this idea of a sex maniac who suddenly becomes rational enough to spare his cousin. No, this murder was committed by a different person, for a different motive, and disguised cunningly and with great thoroughness to look like one of the series.''

''But if Emilia Strozzi was not Vanucci's mistress, why did she not deny it when I asked?''

''You accused her?'' Ciampi asked. ''What did she say?''

''She would not confirm or deny. It was beneath her dignity, she said.''

''In other words, she confirmed, but was she perhaps lying?'' Ciampi though for a long time. ''There is a conspiracy of silence at the Villa Salvadori, involving the gardeners, who are all related to each other, and la Strozzi. They know something about this kidnapping that they have not told me, and now it appears that you have been deceived about the murder of Vanucci. Let us keep in touch, we are pursuing different aspects of the same investigation.''

Sitting in his office at headquarters, Ciampi put his ideas in order. He had a shrewd idea of what lay behind the false kidnapping, and had to choke back self-reproach for not having thought of it before. Should he share this new insight with placid, blond Barbetti, who sat at his desk in a corner? No. So far, it was only an inspired guess. He sent Barbetti on an errand to get rid of him, and applied himself to the telephone.

Like policemen the world over, he had many useful acquaintances in the shady world between legitimate business and crime, and he was on first-name terms with them. But for once, they had little to tell him.

"I am sorry, Alessandro. I have heard nothing" . . . "No, Sandro. Nothing recently" . . . "There was something a few months ago in Florence, but quite minor" . . . "The usual small arrangements that happen all the time, Sandro. Nothing deserving your attention."

His most reliable informant was Pietro Vezzano. Ciampi had left him till last because, being higher placed, he could often be used to check wild rumours peddled to Ciampi by the others.

"How long ago, Sandro?"

"Three or four months, perhaps," Ciampi replied.

"Something quite major?"

"So it seems, Pietro. You have heard something?"

"Yes. Only a rumor. It seems that the negotiations were very difficult and came to nothing."

"I would like to hear more of this," said Ciampi. But nothing more could be said on the telephone. "Can we lunch?"

"One moment. Yes, I am free."

"One o'clock at the usual place?"

"With pleasure, but I warn you that what I know is very vague."

And I know nothing really, I am only guessing, Ciampi thought.

An hour later he was speeding down the *autostrada* to their usual place: the service area between Lucca and Pisa, where two people carrying trayfuls of food in the *auto-servizio* could settle at the same table without necessarily being acquainted. When Ciampi heard more about the "negotiations that came to nothing" he became too tense to eat, he knew he was on the right track.

"Can you give me a name?" he asked.

"It will be difficult. But I will try."

"Please. I must have a name. Without that, I can do nothing."

Back at the Villa Salvadori that afternoon, he confronted the gardeners yet again, then tackled Emilia Strozzi. "Emilia, I do not believe you. In particular I do not believe that you were the mistress of the murdered Andrea Vanucci."

"What it pleases you to believe or not to believe does not concern me."

"Describe to me the scene. It is February. You and Andrea Vanucci are lying together on a blanket in the woods. You are making love. The murderer appears, then what?"

"*Porco mondo*! That I, a respectable woman, should be asked such a question!"

"If you want to be treated as a respectable woman, you must admit the truth. The story of your affair with Vanucci was an invention. He was not the victim of a sex maniac. He was killed because he was too greedy and would not agree to fair shares. And you helped to murder him."

"No! I know nothing of his death."

"So. You were not his mistress, that story is an invention, is that right?"

"Vanucci was my lover, but when he was killed I was not there."

"He was killed, then, in a situation suggestive of a lovers' meeting, but you were not present?"

Throughout the interrogation they had always got stuck at this point. Ciampi was convinced that the gardeners had murdered Vanucci. They had invented a love affair for Emilia to cover up their crime and pass it off as another episode in a long-running series of sex murders. "According to Enrico Fabbri," he said, "you invited Vanucci to meet you secretly at the villa on the pretext of a further discussion about his claim to too large a share in your enterprise. Enrico says his father and cousin killed him on the doorstep when he arrived."

"Enrico said that? No, it is a trick of yours, I don't believe it."

She was right, Enrico had said nothing of the kind. But his discomfort when this version was put to him had convinced Ciampi that it was near the truth. He was also convinced that Emilia had gone over to the enemy. Saddled by the gardeners with a non-existent lover, she had been furious at the slur on her good name, and had provided the kidnappers with a key to the Greek Temple. Knowing when the helicopter was due to arrive, she had made sure that the tourists were safely penned up in the secret garden at the crucial moment.

"The tourists were very late for their appointment, isn't that so?" Ciampi insisted. "You had to hurry them round the sights of the garden with indecent brutality in order to get them into the secret garden in time. Even so, they were a little late and the helicopter had to hover till everything was ready."

"Listen, *Signor Commissario*," said Emilia wearily. "Some foreign tourists were kidnapped while they were visiting the garden here. That is all that happened and we had no part in it. These other things you accuse us of exist only as obsessions in your head."

Ciampi had told Barbetti to make an enquiry in the village, then come back to the villa to pick him up.

"Your guess was right, *capo*," said Barbetti as they met outside the formidable gate. "According to Vanucci's brother, who keeps the wine-shop, Vanucci did some building work last autumn at the Villa Salvadori."

"Did you ask him what repair work Vanucci had done at the villa?"

"Yes, but he did not know the details."

"Then we must ask someone who does," said Ciampi, and rang the bell again. Presently Emilia appeared, looking furious. "What now?" she demanded, scowling.

Asked what work Vanucci had done at the villa, Emilia wanted to know what business that was of his. Driven into a corner, she admitted that he had repaired the vaulted roof on the underground passage leading from the house to the secret garden. This had been done on the instructions of the

135

owner, the Marchese Morandi, because the terrace above showed signs of collapsing into it.

"There is something she did not tell us," said Ciampi as he and Barbetti drove back to headquarters, "but which I discovered earlier today in the municipal library at Lucca. Until recently, this passage was blocked up; in a book which was published two years ago there is a photograph of the secret garden at the Villa Salvadori which shows no trace of the entrance to the tunnel."

"It is strange that she made no mention of this," said Barbetti.

"Strange, and significant. Consider the sequence of events. In the autumn Vanucci unblocks the secret passage, to get access to the vault which he is to repair. In February he is murdered. Also in February, the whole place is put in a state of siege, with guard dogs everywhere, trip-wires to set off an alarm system, all the men sleeping with shot-guns at the ready, allegedly to protect them all from intruders. The Greek Temple acquires a new lock. And what did this suggest to me?"

"I do not know, *capo*," said Barbetti.

"It suggested that I should telephone Pietro Vezzano, and ask for information."

"Vezzano! Yes, *capo*, I begin to see."

"And when he tells me that yes, there is activity in the Lucca area of the type I have in mind, I conclude that all the questions that have tormented us for days can now receive their answers."

Barbetti fell silent, thinking. "Yes *capo*. I think that is so."

It was the last full day of the tour, and Nigel Monk used it to give full rein to his malicious tendency to manipulate people and slide out of responsibility for the uncomfortable consequences for others.

The morning had been left free for shopping, but a number

136

of Farthingaleites had been impressed by Nigel Monk's propaganda for the salutary effects of Montecatini Terme's mud baths, and were up to their necks in debilitating mud before they realized that Monk himself had no intention of joining them in it and was enjoying their discomfiture. He was active again that afternoon, when the programme included a visit to a Florentine villa in an advanced state of decay, with a beautiful but overgrown garden, whose elderly owner had retired for good into a nursing home. The elegant bachelor from Norfolk was delighted with it, and Monk, seizing the opportunity, hypnotised him temporarily into believing that buying and restoring it would be an enjoyable pastime. He was already asking where the owner's lawyers were to be found when Paolo Benedetti drew attention to dry-rot, woodworm and faulty foundations, and pulled him back from the brink of a bottomless financial pit.

On the following day, Farthingale Tours had a full day's program before catching an evening plane to London. At the Villa Mansi, Celia found herself contemplating yet another bed allegedly slept in by Napoleon.

"Many ladies living near Lucca prepared huge beds for that tiny man," Paolo murmured. "But the hopes connected with these beds were not always fulfilled."

"What was Napoleon doing in these parts?" asked Celia, whose grasp of continental history was shaky.

"He was fighting the Austrians and setting up the Cisalpine Republic and taxing the people something terrible and stealing away all our art treasure to Paris, and making his sister Elisabeth Baccioci to be Grand Duchess of Lucca."

"All of which left him no time to pop into all these beds," said Celia.

Paolo smiled, but he was not his usual lively self. He had spent most of the previous evening being questioned by the police.

Later, out in the grounds, Celia and Jane were admiring

137

a stately garden pool* with a balustrade round it, fed by a water staircase in which the water came out of the mouths of slavering dogs.

"Why d'you think they were questioning Paolo?" Jane asked anxiously.

"Goodness knows. He can't have anything to do with it, he wasn't at the dinner-table when Mrs. Hanson said her piece."

"Besides, he's much too nice," Jane added.

"I'll try to find out something about it when I see Commissario Ciampi this afternoon."

The tour program included a free afternoon sightseeing in Pisa before the party caught their plane. Ciampi had left a message for Celia, asking her to call on him for a farewell interview before she went home. In due course the coach joined dozens of others jostling for a parking place, and deposited Farthingale Tours near the Cathedral and Leaning Tower. She had rejected with horror his offer to send a car to collect her from the coach, foreseeing awkward questions from the other Farthingaleites about where she was going and why. Looking forward with interest to another chat with him, she set out on foot, guidebook in hand, to the Law Courts, where they were to meet.

When she arrived she was shown into an office containing two men: Ciampi, and a superior being who sat behind an imposing desk.

"Judge Merlini, the examining magistrate to whom I report," Ciampi explained without enthusiasm. "It is necessary for you to make a deposition before him."

The two relevant volumes of *Spotlight* were open on the desk at the photographs of James Vincent and Paula Martin, and Celia duly deposed that to the best of her knowledge, Paula Martin and James Vincent were identical with persons who had passed themselves off as Ethel and Edward Hanson.

---

*It is alleged that one of the Mansis, a "very merry widow," bathed daily in this pool in fulfillment of a pact with the devil to preserve her beauty.

This was translated into Italian for the benefit of the magistrate, who had no English, but seemed to want to settle down for a comfortable chat with Celia, with Ciampi acting as interpreter.

But Ciampi spat out something in Italian and a fierce argument followed, from which Celia gathered only that the two men loathed each other. Ciampi won it, and ushered Celia out of the office.

"I reminded him that you have to catch your flight to London," he explained, suppressing a grin of triumph. "If he insisted on taking part in the discussion, hours would have passed while everything was translated into Italian for his benefit, and you would have missed your plane. Come, let me offer you some coffee, and I will explain to you the progress we have made."

He sat her down in a café in a quiet square, and began. "There is first a misconception which must be removed. We have decided that this is not a Black Power crime."

Celia refrained from saying that she herself had pointed out this obvious fact to him shortly after the event.

"The two black men who shadowed your group were hired by the criminals," Ciampi went on, "to draw attention to themselves and plant in your minds the idea that the kidnapping was the work of African terrorists. No, the motives for the crime were quite different, and—ah, here comes someone whom I have asked to join us and help me with my explanations."

Approaching their table was a tall, thin grey-haired man who had the weary expression of one who has experienced everything and does not expect to be surprised. Ciampi introduced him as Dottore Petroni of the *Ministero per i Beni Culturali ed Ambientali*.

"I am privileged," said Petroni, "to meet a very intelligent and charming lady who has made it possible to reach some conclusions concerning this unusual case."

"Forgive me," said Celia. "What does your ministry do and how are you involved in this matter?"

"My friend the Commissario can explain, Signora."

"Many years ago," Ciampi began, "a very wise old policeman told me that sometimes one crime could be committed as a cover for another. He was correct. It has happened in this case. The so-called kidnapping was, as you might say, a pseudo-event. The true reason for introducing a helicopter into the grounds of the Villa Salvadori was quite different. As you know, the villa and its garden are heavily defended, with guard dogs and gardeners with shotguns. The helicopter was used to penetrate these defences, in order to steal the object which was being defended."

"But I don't understand," said Celia. "If you steal something, you steal it. Why pretend that you're committing quite a different crime?"

"Because the object being defended was stolen. Thieves in a helicopter were stealing from thieves on the ground. Neither set of thieves could afford to let it become known that the object existed. The presence of the helicopter had to be accounted for in some other way."

"I'm sorry, I'm still bewildered, Commissioner."

"Perhaps you will be less bewildered when I tell you that the object was almost certainly an antique sculpture of some kind, Greek or Roman, which had been found during alterations carried out at the villa in the owners' absence, and that Emilia and the gardeners intended to sell it and divide the proceeds without informing the owners that it had been found."

"And this is my ministry's interest in the case," Petroni put in. "We are responsible for the safe-keeping, in private or public hands, of the nation's cultural heritage, so far as it exists in material form."

"Last year," said Ciampi, "the owners of the villa noticed during their summer holiday that the terrace at the side of the house was subsiding and becoming dangerous. They attributed this, rightly, to the partial collapse of an old passageway lying underneath it which connected the secret garden with the house. They commissioned the local builder, Andrea Vanucci, to make some repairs, which he carried out during last autumn. As you saw when you visited the property, the underground passage has been opened up, and we think that the sculpture at the centre of this affair was found in the blocked passage."

"But who walled it up?" Celia asked, "And why?"

"That is an interesting question, but I have an answer," said Petroni. "According to records in the provincial museum at Lucca, the passageway was not walled up until almost the end of the *settecento*, what you call the eighteenth century. A traveler who wrote a description of the villas near Lucca in 1791 describes it as open then. But an engraving made in the eighteen-twenties shows the entrance to it blocked by the niche with a cupid in it, the arrangement which can be seen in photographs taken in modern times. Now: during Napoleon's Italian campaign from 1795 onwards he was quite ruthless in removing to Paris whatever items of our cultural heritage took his fancy. We are therefore entitled to assume that the owners of the villa used the passageway to conceal a valuable antique work from the depredations of the French Emperor, and disguised the entrance to it with the niche and the cupid."

"And you know what this antique work was?" Celia asked.

"No, unfortunately. There is no record of the Salvadori family possessing such a thing, but they may have acted to oblige a friend, someone with no suitable hiding place available. One or other of the important families still living in a *palazzo* in Lucca would have been in that position, a circumstance which opens up many possibilities. Early in the eighteenth century the great collections made by noble Roman and Florentine families began to be broken up as they became embarrassed for money, the Giustiniani collection for instance, which consisted of about thirteen hundred pieces. Many of the choicer works went to aristocratic English collectors, but a quantity of outstanding items must have remained in Italian hands. The same applies

141

to the Valetta collection in Naples, and the Grimani collection in Venice. It is quite possible that a major work could have been bought by one of the Lucca families and lost sight of."

"Why didn't it reappear after Napoleon was overthrown?" Celia objected.

"By then Salvadori was dead, and his family scattered. Napoleon's sister the Grand Duchess, a lady of great *prepotenza*, had expropriated his villa for the use of one of her relatives. After Napoleon's defeat at Waterloo, it lay empty for some years, and was then lived in by one of the Bourbon-Palmas, who had been granted the Duchy of Lucca by the Congress of Vienna. By then, everyone who knew about the treasure in its secret hiding place would have been dead."

After thinking for a moment Celia said: "But so far all this is only conjecture. You have no hard evidence that anything whatever was found in the underground passage."

It was Ciampi's turn to reply. "I have been making enquiries among informants who are in contact with the art underworld. Rumors were circulating shortly before Christmas of a major find available for clandestine export. But according to my source, the negotiations with intermediaries broke down. The price asked by the finders was excessive, in the sense that it did not allow a sufficient margin of profit for the intermediaries over and above their expenses, which are of course considerable. So also are the difficulties of obtaining a respectable price. There is the question of provenance—"

"I'm sorry, could you explain that?" Celia interrupted.

"It is very simple," said Petroni. "Some account has to be given of where the work has come from, and why it is available for sale without any country claiming the right to give, or more probably refuse, an export license. If it is a bronze, they will say it was fished up from the middle of the Adriatic, well outside Italian and Yugoslav territorial waters, so that it belongs to nobody. This is said only because it is necessary to say something that cannot be disproved, no one is expected to believe it. With a work in marble provenance is more difficult, because marble deteriorates badly in salt water. It preserves well when buried in a *palude di torba*, how do you call it?—"

"A bog of peat," said Ciampi.

"—But unfortunately there are no extra-territorial bogs of peat. So they have to say 'from a private collection in Switzerland', because not all the Swiss secrets are in banks. When Switzerland or the Adriatic are mentioned, everyone knows that the work has been stolen, or at least exported illegally from its country of origin, but that is only the beginning. Then comes the next difficulty. Everyone assumes that a work with such a disreputable provenance is probably a fake. Before some museum can be found that is willing to part with a million or more pounds for it, experts have to be persuaded to pronounce it genuine, and that can be expensive. Even then the question will not be settled, because of the experts who have not been offered any persuasion, and therefore proclaim loudly that on the contrary it is a fake. In the end someone will whisper in the ear of a museum director that this work was found walled up in an underground passage at the Villa Salvadori near Lucca, but please don't say so because of the Italians and their export license. If the museum director believes this, he pays the four or five million dollars. But after all this trouble and expense, there is very little of it left for la Strozzi and the gardeners."

"Four or five million dollars," Celia echoed. "That seems an awful lot."

"Prices have gone crazy, thanks to the American museums. In view of the trouble and expense taken by the thieves to secure it, we must, I think, assume that the work is an important one, probably by an Athenian master of the fourth or fifth centuries. A later Graeco–Roman work would not command a high enough price to make the operation worthwhile."

"Do not forget," said Ciampi, "that one of the major claimants to a share was Vanucci, the builder who did the work on the underground passage. But Emilia Strozzi, the housekeeper, and the three gardeners inevitably knew of the find, and demanded shares of whatever price might be offered. When they found that the total of their demands was excessive and could not be met, they reduced the total bill by murdering Vanucci. This happened in February, and immediately afterwards they put in place the guard dogs and other precautions at the villa."

"But if they'd murdered Vanucci," Celia objected, "why did they need to put the villa into a state of siege?"

"Here we must guess a little. Vanucci, the ringleader in the affair, was a simple village craftsman. To succeed, he had to make a contact with people in the ambiguous section of the international antique market. We are convinced that he did so, for we now know from enquiries in the village that on two occasions in January he visited the villa in the company of a person corresponding to that description."

"Nicolaes Martens," said Dr. Petroni. "A Dutchman dealing in the international antique market. Suspected many times of serious irregularities, but suspicion is not proof."

"He has been the brain behind several affairs of this kind," Ciampi added. "All of them ingenious, and some of them so elaborate that they ended in a fiasco. But because Martens always remained in the background and left the execution to others, it has always proved impossible to convict him."

"How d'you know he's involved in this case?" Celia asked.

"The police records show that he stayed at a hotel in Lucca on two occasions in December, no doubt for the purpose of visiting the Villa Salvadori and evaluating Vanucci's find. We suspect that Vanucci and Martens decided to steal the work, and avoid sharing the proceeds with la Strozzi and the gardeners. It is even possible that Vanucci was murdered during a failed attempt at theft. But the danger would not have ended with his death, for he was dealing with people who were no more ready than he was to give shares to others. For reasons of this kind la Strozzi and the gardeners took their precautions, which were formidable enough to defeat any normal attempt to steal the work. But as we know, Martens and his accomplices found a clever way round the difficulty.''

"One thing puzzles me," said Celia after thinking for a moment. "The thieves drop from the sky in a helicopter. How do they know where to find the statue? The gardeners might have moved it from wherever Martens saw it.''

"Martens had an ally among the staff at the villa. For reasons which need not concern you, we are sure it was Emilia Strozzi. She even supplied him with a key to the Greek Temple.''

Celia was puzzled. "In that case, why the helicopter and the false kidnapping and the whole elaborate carry-on? If Martens had an ally at the villa, surely, they could have found an easier way?''

"Not easily. Remember, three gardeners live at the villa and sleep with loaded shotguns beside them. Suppose that la Strozzi succeeds in drugging five Alsatians and three gardeners, and opening the gates to admit a vehicle, because the statue is heavy, and cannot be carried very far. What explanation does she give to the others in the morning? Would they not deal with her as they did with Vanucci?''

"I suppose so, Commissario. And I see now why it was necessary to shut up the gardeners in the Greek Temple.''

Ciampi nodded vigorously. "The statue was in the Greek Temple. The programme of the pseudo-event, that is to say of the kidnapping, had to provide an excuse for breaking into it, so that we who investigated afterwards should not know that something had been taken out of it to the helicopter and stolen away.''

"But you would have known!" she cried. "The Prices were there. If they saw whatever it was being carried into the helicopter, they'd have told you.''

"Precisely. So now another of our questions can be answered. We know why Mr. and Mrs. Price had to be killed, while the gardeners, who witnessed the same event, did not. They could be relied on to remain, as you might say, mum concerning their guilty secret."

"There's a snag about all this," said Celia. "Unless and until you know what bit of Italy's cultural heritage has been stolen, you can hardly claim it back when it turns up on the international art market."

"Unfortunately that is so," said Petroni.

"In that case," Celia reasoned, "your best hope is to discover which of my suspects is the kidnapper's confederate on the tour: the Enderby-Scotts, the Carstairs ménage, Major Gatling or Mr. Monk."

Ciampi fiddled with his tiny coffee-cup, as if embarrassed by what he was about to say. "We are very grateful to you, Signora, for the help you have given us. But it will not be necessary to investigate your suspicions, because we know that the hostagetakers' confederate on the tour was Paolo Benedetti, the courier."

"Oh no! Surely not."

"I am afraid this disappoints you, he is a very sympathetic and, as you might say, dishy young man. But the evidence is clear. He is a member of a formerly wealthy family, reduced to earning a precarious living in the antique trade. We have questioned his employer, who denies everything. He is an antique dealer of good reputation, and we suspect that Benedetti was recruited by Martens without the firm's knowledge."

"But—"

"One moment, Signora. We have questioned his *amorosa*, his girlfriend so to speak, and know that he persuaded her to let him take her place as courier on the tour."

"He made no secret of that. It was because she'd broken her leg," said Celia.

"No, the broken leg was an invention, to deceive the organizers of the tour in London. He told the young woman that as this was an expensive tour of rich people with artistic interests, it would be an opportunity to make acquaintances who would be useful to him in his profession. For that reason she let him take her place.''

Celia thought hard. ''If you're right, Commissioner, the man involved in stealing a work of art from the Villa Salvadori just happened to have a girlfriend who could give up to him her place as courier on this particular tour. Isn't that too much of a coincidence to be credible?''

''We think, Signora, that it was not a coincidence. Men sometimes acquire a girlfriend for reasons of temporary convenience and not for their plastic qualities. You find this difficult to accept, no doubt you took a favorable view of this handsome young man. But are you surprised that the young woman in question succumbed to his attractions?''

Celia swallowed her outrage at this sexist innuendo, and managed to reply calmly. ''But it can't be Benedetti. He wasn't at the dinner-table when Mrs. Hanson made her speech.''

Ciampi made another embarrassed dive into his tiny coffee cup. ''I hope you will not be offended if I tell you that we think you are mistaken about this. The incident at the dinner-table does not necessarily bear the interpretation you have put on it. We have no evidence that Mrs. Hanson was connected in any way with the theft of the Marchesa's silver, any of the tourists could have taken it. One supposes that the threat of a search persuaded the *cleptomane* to return it, or else that the husband or wife of the *cleptomane* did so, as often happens in these cases.''

He rose, to bring the interview to an end. ''I apologize for keeping you away for so long from the touristic delights of Pisa, which I hope you will now enjoy. But Dr. Petroni and I felt we owed you a debt to explain to you in detail the background to this case, and to show you why we do not think it appropriate to make any further enquiries in England.''

''But there is a British angle,'' Celia protested. ''The

tour operator was British. The Vincents are British. They may have to return to England, they have a handicapped child and I think they left him there.''

''Those matters will be attended to as necessary, though the British police believe that the Vincents are in Spain, and we are having enquiries made there. What I meant to say is, the solution of this case does not lie in England.''

''Then where does it lie?'' asked Celia, much put out.

''In the apartment of Dr. Nicolaes Martens, above his antique gallery in Amsterdam,'' said Petroni.

''But how can you be sure?''

''I am almost sure. In any case, there is a very simple reason why the stolen object will not reappear in Britain. The British laws on the export of cultural property are as strict as our own. Any important work of art suddenly 'discovered' on British soil would be worth barely half what it would fetch on the open market, because of the almost impossibility of obtaining an export license. It will appear from Switzerland or the middle of the Adriatic, of that we can be sure.''

''So you can return to your home in the green county of Sussex,'' Ciampi added as he ushered her out of the café, ''and forget about these sad events which have spoilt your Italian holiday.''

Celia was aghast. She had been pleasantly surprised by the way Ciampi had taken her into his confidence, and had encouraged Petroni to do so. She assumed that he would ask her to keep her eyes open on his behalf when she got home. But she had misread him. This whole long rigmarole had been planned to lead up to exactly the opposite conclusion: there was no British angle, she must leave it to the experts and mind her own business. As he stood facing her in the street and waiting for her to go, his mouth was smiling but his eyes were not. She was being dismissed, and it made her very angry.

❧ EIGHT ❧

Celia found everything in apple-pie order at Archerscroft Nurseries. The last orders of late-flowering spray chrysanthemums had been dispatched, the seed beds and frame-yard were aggressively weed-free and last year's crosses among the old-fashioned border pinks had produced an interesting color break with an almost black fringed border.

"So you was wrong," Bill Wilkins told her in triumph. "You thought we'd have red spider in the greenhouses and bindweed in the frame-yard soon as your back was turned, and we'd be bankrupt. Oh yes you did, Celia, you nearly didn't go. I had to stuff you into that plane like a terrified colt into a horse box."

"Well I'm back now, so let's get down to work," she said. "That new lot of hellebore seedlings need pricking out."

"That can wait, you got to confess to me first. You been on the prowl."

"Oh dear, how did you know?"

"Oh Celia, it was in all the papers and on the telly, how kidnappers had taken the wrong hostages off of your tour. I knew you'd never keep your nose out of that lot." He sat forward eagerly. "Come on then, tell."

She told him the full story, and added: "So you see, almost all the prowling was done by the Italian police. And when I said I thought they were wrong to suspect Paolo Benedetti, they went terribly male chauvinist and said I was an adorable little goose who'd been taken in by a plausible young man with a pretty face."

"And had you?" Bill asked.

"I've never been taken in by your pretty face, have I?"

He grinned, remembering some of their rows. "Oh no, Celia."

Bill was young enough to be her son. She had made it clear to him long ago that despite his striking good looks she had no interest in him, except as a valued employee and friend.

"Be serious now," he said. "Why don't you want Paolo Benedetti as a suspect?"

"He was quite open about being connected with the antique trade. And he didn't spend the evenings at the hotel, he went home to his girlfriend. So he couldn't have doctored my drink, and he wasn't at the dinner-table during the fuss over the stolen jug. I tried to argue about it with Ciampi, but there was no way of getting through to him. I think I'd upset him earlier on by pointing out something fairly obvious that he hadn't thought of first, and after that everything I said was wrong."

"They say there's no British angle. Are they right?"

"On the main point, I think they must be. The statue or whatever it is can't have been brought to England to be 'discovered' because of the tax laws and the stiff conditions for export licenses. Anyway, I've been told to mind my own business. I'll just have to forget the whole thing."

"OK then Celia. Let's have a look at them hellebore seedlings."

For over a month they worked hard. It was a busy time of year, and they had to nurse the stock through a spell of very hot weather. Celia's only information about the case came from press reports. The kidnappers had gone on pestering Mrs. Waters by telephone for a week or two, insisting that the people they were holding were her parents, and that she and the police were pretending otherwise with the help of the corrupt capitalist media. In a final phone call, a man who sounded either drunk or beside himself from fury, had announced that the hostages had been killed and dumped in a lake, and their blood was on Mrs. Waters' head. Ciampi seemed to have kept his own counsel and said as little as possible to the media. The identification of the Vincents with the Hansons was the one card up his sleeve in his battle of wits with the kidnappers, and he had kept it there.

Left in ignorance of this vital piece of information, the media were prepared to believe that the kidnappers had made a genuine mistake in identification, and on realizing it, had killed their hostages in a fit of embarrassed rage. But the crime reporters had been snuffling round the Villa Salvadori like bloodhounds. Faced with a very peculiar kidnapping, a house mysteriously guarded by savage dogs, a housekeeper and gardeners who scowled and would not talk, a series of brutal sex murders and a village buzzing with rumours, they had constructed a variety of scenarios, each more lurid than the last.

Celia, excluded from the action, was feeling very frustrated. She had to apologize to Bill several times for snapping at him. He became snappish too, infected by her mood.

"What's wrong, Celia?" he demanded in the middle of a busy morning. "You been like a camel with a belly-ache all week."

"Oh dear, I'm sorry if I was shrewish. You know how an unsolved puzzle nags at me."

"Then solve it."

"How can I? It's hopeless."

"No it isn't, there's lots of leads you can follow up. You can check on your dinner-table suspects and make sure they're who they say they are. You can find out what you can about the Vincents from their agent; all actors have an agent, don't they? Go on, you're no use to the business while you're in this state."

"We're too busy."

"No we're not."

Celia considered. It was late June. The worst of the early-summer rush was over, everything was well in hand. She could spare a little time, perhaps. When next she had to go up to the Horticultural Hall, she would look in on the Vincents' agent.

So on a hot afternoon in early July she found herself in Bloomsbury, toiling up a staircase which smelt of cats to a top-floor office inhabited by Elaine Bundry, Theatrical Agent.

She was a hard-bitten lady in her sixties, and listened with raised eyebrows to Celia's claim to be an old friend of the Vincents' who had lost touch. Did she know where they were working, and would she be willing to forward a letter?

"Private enquiry agent, are you dear?" she asked when Celia had finished.

"No! Why?"

"The police were here back in May, asking the same sort of thing." She studied Celia doubtfully. "You don't look like a gumshoe, I must say. You in the theatre? No? Pity. You've got the figure for it and you move well."

"D'you know why the police were asking about the Vincents?" Celia asked.

"They didn't let on. Routine enquiries, they said. I don't know who you are or whether you're on the level, but I don't mind telling you what I told them. Jimmy Vincent came in here back in May and said they'd come into money unexpectedly, a cousin had died or something, and they were going to settle abroad."

"You don't know where?"

"No. There was a postcard from Torremolinos back in May, but with no address on."

"I suppose they took Tom with them?" Celia asked.

"No. Jimmy decided it was better to leave him where he was till they'd found a place of their own where there were facilities for a handicapped child."

"Which will be never, if Jimmy has anything to do with it?" Celia suggested.

Elaine Bundry made a doubtful face. "Paula's devoted to Tom. If it came to a crunch, I don't know which of them would win."

"I'd like to check up, and visit Tom if he's still in the home. Where is it?"

"In Kent, I think she said."

"You don't remember its name?"

"Sorry, no, but it was a churchy sort of name. I think it was run by nuns."

In a telephone box near the British Museum she rang a charitable society concerned with the welfare of handicapped children. It was happy to supply her with the phone numbers of homes in Kent which would be suitable for her Down's syndrome child. She'd like the little boy to be in a religious atmosphere, was there one run by nuns? Yes there was, St. Saviour's Hospice in Maidstone, highly recommended and convenient for visiting as it was five minutes' walk from the station.

A call to St. Saviour's Hospice confirmed that it had a Thomas Vincent in residence. Were visitors allowed? Of course. At any reasonable time.

Was the present time reasonable, Celia asked herself. On the whole, yes. It would mean getting back to Archerscroft very late, but at least the chore would be over.

Having bought some crayons and a child's drawing-book on the way to Victoria Station, she took the train to Maidstone and presented herself at a grim Victorian building of greyish brick. But for a statue of the Virgin Mary in its front garden it could have been mistaken for a prison. Inside, though, all was light and color and cheerfulness. Tom Vincent, pointed out to her in a noisy group of children, was about eight years old and an engaging little boy, less abnormal looking than some of the others. He came over to her at once, was delighted with the crayons and made her take turns with him at drawing things. Presently other children came over to see what was going on, and Celia found herself drawing aircraft and motor cars for the entertainment of a largish group.

When their concentration began to flag, she went to discuss Tom with the nun in charge. "His parents are abroad, I believe?"

"That is so, yes."

"Forgive me for being inquisitive, but I hope they don't intend to abandon him. I know Mrs. Vincent liked to have him with them whenever she could, but if they're abroad that may not be possible. D'you think they intend to leave him with you for the rest of his life?"

The atmosphere cooled markedly. "May I ask, Mrs. Grant, why you are interesting yourself in this matter?"

Celia made an unconvincing claim to be a friend of the family. But this got her no further and she withdrew.

Back at Archerscroft, she reported her findings to Bill, who said: "Fine. And now you can find out if all your dinner-table suspects are who they say they are."

"How? I haven't even got their addresses. I was relying on Ciampi to give me them before I left, but after he'd choked me off like that I couldn't."

"There's *Who's Who*. There's phone directories. Go on, Celia, don't be so feeble."

Am I being feeble, Celia asked herself, or just realistic? Was it really worth toiling round the countryside investigating the backgrounds of the people she suspected?

"Yes it is, Celia," Bill insisted. "You'll never settle down till you get to the bottom of this."

"But the bottom of it isn't here, damn you. It's in Switzerland or the middle of the Adriatic."

"Not if you're right about what was going on at the dinner-table that night."

"But am I right?" Celia murmured.

"You don't get that sort of thing wrong, Celia. You gone and lost your nerve, that's the trouble."

"No. The real trouble is, you've worked yourself up into a giddy state of curiosity about this thing, much worse than me."

He grinned. "OK, I have. What of it?"

"So I run around looking into a lot of dead-ends while you sit back and enjoy."

"Go on, Celia. Go to the public library and look these people up. You know you want to really."

"You beast, stop treating me like a pig being driven to market."

Nevertheless, she did as she was told, and came back from the library with a closely written sheet of extracts from telephone directories and works of reference.

"Let's see what we got here," said Bill, running his eye over it. "Here's one you can check out on the phone. What's the use of having a well-informed stockbroker in love with you if you don't use him when you want to know something?"

She resisted the idea. Harry Wintringham, the highly placed former admirer who managed her financial affairs, was now a happily married friend. "It's not fair to exploit him like this," she protested.

"Yes it is. Go on, ring him."

Under protest, she made the call. "Harry? It's Celia."

After some warmly welcoming preliminaries he asked what he could do for her.

"I'm up to my old tricks, Harry, I'm afraid."

He was all concern. "Don't tell me gunmen have been using you for target practice again?"

"No, not this time. Tell me about a family called Enderby-Scott. I've looked them up, and there seem to be a lot of them with directorships and so on in the city, mostly in insurance. I'm specially interested in R. J. Enderby-Scott."

"Ah yes. That's the grandson, very clever. He's just

155

taken over as chairman of the family merchant bank.''

"Rich?''

"My dear Celia, they all are.''

"What puzzles me is, R. J. is the only one who isn't in *Who's Who*.''

"There's a reason for that. He's married to poor Cecily Gaveston's daughter. You probably remember the case?''

"No, Harry. Tell me.''

"It was about fifteen years ago. Cecily Gaveston was kidnapped while she was on holiday in Corsica. There was no kidnap insurance in those days and these things weren't handled expertly. The husband paid over a huge sum in ransom, only to find that she was dead. Awful for the daughter, losing her mother like that, and of course she's terrified that the same thing might happen to her. That's why they keep a very low profile, you'll find very little about them in any of the directories.''

She thanked him and reported her findings to Bill. "There's one of our suspect couples looking like non-starters. They said nothing about themselves because they didn't want anyone to discover that they were rolling in money. And when the kidnapping happened, it shattered them, as it would anyone with that sort of tragedy in the background.''

"OK, so we forget about them for the moment," Bill conceded. "Who do we try next?''

"Slave driver,'' Celia moaned.

"What about this Major Gatling? He looks the likeliest.''

"I suppose so. He's alleged to have a secret service background.''

"And didn't you say he deals in garden sculptures?''

"In a refined sort of way, yes.''

"Well there you are then. Off you go to Berkshire tomorrow to check him out.''

No, Celia thought, Major Gatling doesn't belong here. There's some mistake, I've come to the wrong place.

She had had her doubts as soon as she saw the entry in the trade directory. But Major H. N. Gatling figured in the Farthingale Tours list as living in Berkshire, and Gatling's Garden Stores was the only Berkshire firm in the trade directory which claimed to sell sculpture.

Gatling's Garden Stores occupied a corner site on a main road in the Berkshire commuter belt, and its stock in trade was adapted to the tastes of the most unfastidious Berkshire commuters. Glaring white plastic urns and flower boxes stood on paving of tinted concrete, surrounded by low walls of reconstituted stone in a variety of unpleasant colors. Hectic flower patterns adorned the cushions of the garden chairs and the matching umbrellas over the garden tables. If the allegedly "spooky" Major used this panorama of bad taste as cover for some clandestine activity, it could hardly have to do with stolen works of art. The only "sculptures" on view were of concrete, and represented chubby infants clutching dolphins and coyly naked ladies with birdbaths at their feet. A stolen Greek or Roman statue would have stood out among them like a very sore thumb.

Celia was tempted to drive straight home. But she would get merry hell from Bill if she failed to investigate thoroughly, so she picked her way past fibreglass goldfish pools and artificial waterfalls into the shack-like sales office.

Major Gatling was sitting behind a desk. "Hullo Major," she said. "You forgot to give me your business card, but I've tracked you down."

His dismay bordered on panic.

"I'm looking for a garden sculpture, remember?" she added. "For my rose garden."

He stood up behind the desk. There were grease stains on his trousers and his shirt hung out over them. His soldierly chest had vanished and been replaced by a beer belly, the natural result of not wearing a corset. The transformation embarrassed Celia as much as it did him.

"Introduce me, Harry dear," said a voice from behind

her. She spun round and saw a middle-aged woman sitting in a wheelchair.

"Oh, yes," said the Major unhappily. "My wife. This is Mrs. . . . Miss . . ."

"Grant," said Celia. "I met your husband in Italy."

"Yes dear, I guessed that." After they had conversed for a few minutes she pointed to a mass of paperwork on her lap. "You talk business with Harry and I'll get on with the accounts."

Celia pretended to be considering whether one of the concrete ladies with birdbaths at their feet would do for her rose garden, objected to the bulbous babies as too small, and began dithering about among plastic urns as a possible alternative. She was baffled. Was this dismal commercial enterprise a front for something, and if so what? She saw no way of finding out, and was about to give up and leave when Mrs. Gatling rolled her wheelchair to the door of the sales shack and called her. "Don't run away yet dear, it's coffee-time. Do stay and have some with us and chat for a bit. Harry dear, would you?"

Harry disappeared into the back premises of the shack and could be heard busying himself with a kettle.

Mrs. Gatling lowered her voice. "Don't call him 'Major', dear, he isn't one. He only says he is on holiday."

"But he must have been in the army. He knows so much about it."

"Yes dear, he was a driver for years, drove all the high-ups, General Carver, the lot, and he picked up all the gossip. You mustn't worry about his little games, he has a miserable time most of the year with the worry of the business and me stuck in the wheelchair, so I make him go off on holiday by himself when we can afford it." She put her hand on Celia's. "And while he's away I don't grudge him his little bit of fun."

Outraged at being mistaken for Harry's little bit of fun, Celia downed her coffee and drove back to Archerscroft in a fury. "Why do you make me do these things?" she stormed at Bill. "There's no point. That poor little man has the soul of a plastic gnome, he wouldn't know what to do with the Apollo Belvedere if someone gave it him."

"Never mind, Celia. There's two more suspects to be looked into."

"And what would I find out? That people treat their holiday as a marvelous chance to play-act? That Nigel Monk's a butcher who lives over the shop, or the transvestite butler of an elderly gay? That Lady Carstairs runs a kinky underwear shop in Basingstoke?"

"She sounds very suspicious to me, what with her crude little boyfriend," said Bill.

"Oh surely not. A woman with her anatomy on her mind to that extent can't have much room in her head for anything else, let alone crime."

"Maybe her crude little boyfriend has crime on his mind and not her anatomy."

"Well you're very much mistaken if you think I'm going to toil down to Hampshire to probe her disreputable secrets. Anyway, I can't. I have no conceivable reason for calling on her."

"What about this Nigel Monk, then?"

"He's a half-mad practical joker and I haven't even got his address. Leave me alone, Bill. I've had enough mare's nests for one day, and tomorrow we must pot up five hundred *Aster frikartii* cuttings."

"Celia, I been thinking," said Bill as they worked in the potting shed next morning. "Why don't I go and chat up this Lady Carstairs for you?"

Knowing from the Farthingale Tours list that Lady Carstairs lived in Hampshire, Celia had tracked her down in Winchester with the aid of the telephone directory. "D'you think it's worth it? All that way?"

"I could go Tuesday," Bill urged. "Stop off at Wisley on the way and drop in them eremurus seedlings we said we'd let them have."

"Bill, when it comes to curiosity you're worse than me."

"No point in leaving a job half done. OK about Tuesday?"

Oh no, this can't be right, Bill thought, just as Celia had done. He had imagined from the address that he would find Lady Carstairs in a gracious old-world town house somewhere near Winchester Cathedral. But Temple Mead House turned out to be a hideous stockbroker's Tudor villa, standing back from a busy arterial road in a suburb which seemed to be zoned for light industry. Earth-moving equipment was parked in what had once been its garden, and the building had the run-down look of a house converted into offices. But a large signboard at the entrance read "George Johnson, Ltd, Contractors". It had to be the right place after all. George Johnson was the name of Lady Carstairs' "stepson".

Bill drove in and parked. The front door was open, and a girl in an office marked "Enquiries" told him, when he said he was looking for Lady Carstairs, that she lived "round the back". Picking his way past the contractors' machinery, he found that what had once been the kitchen wing of the house had been turned into a neat cottage with a walled garden.

Bill drove the van up to the cottage and rang the bell. The old lady who answered was white haired and heavily made up, but her clothes were more homely than he had expected from Celia's description, and her glasses were on a string round her neck. By way of pretext for his call he had loaded into the van several trayfuls of an Archerscroft speciality: a strain of old-fashioned cottage pinks collected from gardens in Ireland and crossbred for continuous flowering. He opened the doors at the back to show them to her.

She put on her glasses and peered into the van. "You devilish young man, you're tempting me."

With a different tone of voice, the remark could have been sexily double-edged. But there was no hint of coquetry in her tone or manner, it had not occurred to her that she could be misunderstood. After years of warding off unwelcome invitations to promiscuity, Bill had developed a reliable early-warning system. It told him that Celia had got it wrong. Lady Carstairs was not that sort. She would never have dreamed of treating herself to a holiday fling with a crude young stud.

"How much d'you want for them?" she asked, intent on the pinks.

The normal price was two pounds each. But money seemed to be a consideration, so he brought it down to what he thought she could afford.

"Very well," she said. "I'll take a dozen."

Despite her short-sightedness she had a good eye, and picked out a dozen of the best. Bill carried them through the house for her and out into the little walled garden.

"Oh where, where shall I put them?" she cried. "As you see, my eyes are bigger than my flowerbeds."

Bill was astonished. She had achieved a miracle in a tiny space. Nothing was out of scale. The planting had been done with sound horticultural knowledge and an artist's eye for effective groupings, using always the best forms rather than those easily found in garden centers. Some plants, notably a group of snow-white dwarf eremurus, were not normally available in commerce.

"That's a nice little anthemis," he said to establish his credentials. "Looks nice in front of the veronica."

She looked at him shrewdly. "Ah, and which veronica is it, do you know?"

"With the silver foliage, it must be *cinerea*. You been very clever, using all these small things, instead of filling up with rose bushes and stuff."

She went on testing him out. When he had correctly identified a zantedeschia growing by a small pool, a *Digitalis ambigua* and three varieties of herbaceous potentilla, she asked him rather hesitantly if he would like a coffee.

He accepted, and they sat down in the kitchen to drink

it. "D'you mind me asking you something?" he said. "How come a lady like you who's clever with her garden lives in the back premises of a contractor's yard?"

She looked at him mistily. "Do you believe in miracles?"

"I'm . . . not sure."

"When my poor husband died leaving me penniless, I was saved from misery and starvation by the greatest miracle of all, the astonishing generosity of human nature. George is only my stepson, there is no tie of blood."

"George Johnson, is that? Who runs the yard?"

"He owns it. Such a gifted boy, he started with a loan of five hundred pounds when he was eighteen and built it up from nothing, he inherited his father's flair for business. He found me starving in a back room in Brighton and gave me a wonderful lunch at the Metropole and asked me to come here and keep house for him."

"That's nice," said Bill.

She nodded vigorously. "That was six years ago, and he has been a paragon of kindness itself ever since."

"You've no children of your own?" Bill asked.

"Only one son. He's in America."

"Any grandchildren?"

She hesitated for a moment. "I don't know. I hope so, but we've lost touch."

Her painted face sagged into sadness, but lit up again when George Johnson appeared in the kitchen doorway. "Coffee up, love?"

While she bustled affectionately to get him some, George chatted Bill up, very much the master of the house and the head of a successful business. He was not touring Italy now among a lot of well-heeled snobs. In that company, Bill told himself, a person with his background and habits would look like a very coarse fish out of water.

"I been admiring the garden, it's a real beauty," he said.

George nodded. "She's clever at it. I'm taking her into partnership."

He explained that landscape gardening was an obvious

side-line for his firm. He would supply the earth-moving equipment and she would contribute design sense and horticultural knowledge.

"A revival of the formal garden is overdue, I think," said Lady Carstairs. "Maintenance is no problem if one designs them properly. George and I made an expedition to Italy this spring to look at gardens there, and came back with our heads teeming with ideas. I do think the English gardening style has become rather shapeless and sloppy . . ."

So that was that, Bill thought as she talked on. This odd pair had gone to Italy to look at gardens. Another suspect was out of it.

Half-way back to Archerscroft it occurred to him to wonder: how did a couple called Carstairs with an only son manage to have a stepson called Johnson? Reporting back to Celia, he said: "George must be an illegit."

"In which case, how admirable of him to look after the old lady, and how dreadful of me to have suspected otherwise."

"He's rough, you weren't to know. If his mum was rough and his dad didn't do nothing about him, he'd have been brought up rough."

"You'd think the old lady would try to civilize him a bit."

"Oh no, Celia, he wouldn't want to be civilized. If you're an illegit that's come up from the bottom and done well, you go bloody-minded and stay how you are and despise people that talk posh. What sort of man was his dad, I wonder?"

Celia had looked Lady Carstairs up in Burke's *Baronetage and Knightage*, which stated with a bald lack of detail that she was the widow of Sir Henry Carstairs, who had died in 1980. According to her he had been a businessman, presumably on a largish scale, since his activities had earned him a knighthood. But he had left his widow very badly off, what had happened? Out of curiosity she rang her stock-broking admirer again.

"Henry Carstairs? Of course I remember him, Celia. Had a big stake in South Africa in the days when that sort of thing was considered quite respectable. Knighted 'for public services' which I think meant a big contribution to Conservative party funds."

"Then why did he leave his widow very badly off?"

"Well he would, wouldn't he? It was one of the biggest bankruptcies of the early eighties, a lot of my clients got their fingers burnt. Shot himself, or he'd have gone to prison for fraud."

"D'you remember, Harry, what happened to the family?"

"There was a son, I think. Ran off to America with whatever he could salt away, leaving the widow to face the music."

"How about illegitimate children?"

"Dozens, I should imagine. Henry Carstairs was an out-and-out tomcat, led his poor wife an awful dance."

Celia thanked him for his information and reported to Bill. "So it was all perfectly pure and above-board. George is her husband's illegitimate son who emerged from hiding and came to the rescue after the crash. He's looked after her ever since, and they had a perfectly good reason for going on that tour of Italy together. I suppose it never occurred to either of them that dirty-minded people like me might have other ideas."

"So we got to cross him off, and this Nigel Monk's the only suspect we got left."

"Yes. But he was a complete fool. And I told you, I haven't got his address."

"Oh Celia, that's not like you. How come?"

"I couldn't very well ask people for their addresses at the end of the tour, I was a sort of moral leper cast out from decent society. I'd intended to ask that Italian policeman, but how could I after he brushed me off and said the whole thing had nothing to do with Britain?''

"You can still trace Monk. Ring the tour operator, they'll tell you."

To keep him quiet, she rang Farthingale Tours, who said giving clients' addresses to each other was contrary to their policy, but they would forward a letter.

"Don't give up," Bill urged. "There's the phone directory. What's wrong with that?"

"Only that there are four volumes for Oxfordshire, which is where Monk belongs according to the Farthingale Tours list. There must be half a dozen Monks in each of them."

"With the right initial?"

"Oh. I suppose not."

"Ring all the N Monks then, and ask to speak to Nigel till you get the right one."

"Oh very well, but stop bullying me."

"Go on then. Do it now."

"I can't, till I've been to the library again and copied the numbers from the Oxfordshire directory."

Out of perversity, she spent the next day potting up several hundred primula seedlings, and did not finish till after the library was shut. On the day after that she had to go to London for a show at the Horticultural Hall, which provided an excuse for yet more delay.

After spending the morning sitting in judgment there on late-flowering shrubs, she went to her club to keep a lunch date with Jane Armstrong. When they separated at London Airport after the Italian tour, they had agreed to keep in touch, and this was the first opportunity for a meeting.

Jane was delighted to see her. "Have you got any further with the Hanson problem?"

"Not really. Any action there is must be at the Italian end, except that I've traced Tom, the Down's syndrome son. He's at a home in Maidstone, and likely to stay there. I think Jimmy's persuaded his wife to leave him there permanently."

"Oh, poor little thing. Maidstone's only three stations up the line from home. I could drop in to see him."

"Do, he'd like that. The other interesting development is, Major Gatling turns out to have a guilty secret, but not the one you might expect."

She told Jane the story, which fascinated her. "I see exactly how it could have happened, Celia. Generals gossip to their drivers on long journeys the way women do to their hairdressers. It was a worm's eye view by a very high-level worm. No wonder Dad thought he was a spook."

"Don't tell your parents, Jane. They'll think I went off after the gallant Major on a nymphomaniac manhunt and got a nasty surprise."

She went on to explain that Lady Carstairs and George were cleared of suspicion, and that the Enderby-Scotts were very unlikely starters. "That only leaves Nigel Monk, who's half mad. And I don't even know where he lives."

"Oxfordshire," said Jane promptly.

"I know, but it's huge."

"Somewhere near Bicester."

"Really? Are you sure?"

"Yes. It was while we were at Pisa airport waiting for the plane. He and Mum were talking about restaurants, and he was saying that one of the best restaurants in the world was quite near him in Oxfordshire, and then he sort of choked, as if he'd made a *gaffe*. And Dad said was it the Golden Pheasant in Bicester, because he'd been there when he went shooting with our Oxfordshire cousins. And Monk had to say it was, but he wasn't happy about it and when Dad tried to talk Oxfordshire to him he shied off."

Armed with this information, Celia went back yet again to the public library. With the help of a road atlas and the right volume of the telephone directory, she listed all the Monks living within a ten-mile radius of Bicester. Back at Archerscroft, with Bill urging her on mercilessly, she rang them all. None of them admitted to being Nigel Monk, or knowing anyone of that name. "This is a wild-goose chase," she raged. "I'm wasting no more time on it."

Bill gripped both her hands, a thing he sometimes did when making a solemn pronouncement. "Listen Celia. Was you wrong about what was happening that night at the dinner-table?"

"No! I don't care what anyone says, she was saying she'd do what she was told, and they weren't to persecute her."

"Then why give up?"

"It's hopeless."

"It's not. Nigel Monk's your suspect, the others is all out of it. Don't you give up now."

"There's no one called Nigel Monk living near Bicester."

"Then he was lying when he said that about the restaurant."

"I don't think so. Jane says he had a reaction afterwards, as if he'd given away something he didn't mean to."

"Then Bicester is right, he lives near there, but his name's not Nigel Monk and he was lying when he said it was."

"Oh marvelous, Bill. Very helpful. What do I do now, ring up everyone in the directory and ask if they've pretended to be called Nigel Monk? Now go home and stop bullying me, I've had all I can stand for tonight."

But when she woke at three in the morning, she found herself thinking again about the Monk problem. What sort of man was he, what made him tick? The perverted exercise of power, talking other people into doing silly things. And was Bill right? Did Monk live near Bicester, but under another name? As she tossed and turned, the thought sparked off an idea so fantastic that she could not take it seriously, even in the still watches of the night. In the morning it seemed utterly absurd, and she put it out of her head. On her next shopping trip into town she walked firmly past the library, determined not to go inside and test it out. But curiosity was too strong for her. She turned back and went in.

Now that hardly anyone had their monogram plastered over all their possessions, there was no particular reason why people choosing an alias for themselves should go for one with the same initials as their real name. But people still did it, perhaps out of superstition. Was "Nigel Monk" superstitious? Or was it just a coincidence that he had the same initials as Nicolaes Martens?

Perhaps. But it could hardly be a coincidence that someone called E. G. Martens lived in King's Easton, four miles from Bicester.

Nigel Monk talked people into doing silly things, then stepped clear before he could be blamed for the result. According to Ciampi, Nicolaes Martens had been the brains behind art frauds in which others got their fingers burnt and he went scot-free. Was there a parallel here? Had Nicolaes Martens, alias Nigel Monk, acting from force of habit, exercised on the Farthingaleites in a small way the perverted talent which, on a larger scale, got other people involved in elaborate and ingenious but perhaps risky crimes? This whole complex scheme, the hijacking of the helicopter and the false kidnapping, fitted into the pattern. Nicolaes Martens would watch events from the safe cover of Farthingale Tours under a false name. If anything went wrong, he would be safe. Only the crew of the helicopter would come to grief.

Excited by her discovery, she drove back to Archerscroft in a cheerful and resolute mood and prepared to ring E. G. Martens in Oxfordshire.

"What will you say if your Nigel answers?" Bill asked.

"I shall pretend I want to sell him double-glazing or insurance."

The call was answered by a lady with a very upper-class voice.

"Is Mr. Nicolaes Martens there, please?"

"Nick? No. Why should he be?"

"I believe he's in England at present, and I thought he might be with you?"

"No. If he's in England it's news to me, he was in Amsterdam three days ago. Who wants him?"

"It's about his car insurance. I may have misunderstood; I'll ring Amsterdam again."

She put the phone down and reached for her address book.

"What next?" Bill asked.

"I shall ring everyone I know in Oxfordshire. Was that his sister or his mother or his estranged wife or what? I've got to find out."

Leafing through her address book, she rang a schoolfriend living in the area who was astonished to hear from her, and a nurseryman she had occasional dealings with. Neither of them had heard of anyone called Martens. The next entry that caught her eye was rather daunting. It was the address of a great house only a few miles from King's Easton, where she and Roger had stayed once or twice while Roger was advising the owners about their garden. But that was ten years ago. Even if the noble family remembered her, would they be able to tell her anything about the mother or wife or whatever she was of a crooked antique dealer who lived in Amsterdam?

But Celia's blood was up. She made the call, and the noble lady who answered was gracious. "Mrs. Grant? Of course I remember. How are you, and what are you doing nowadays?"

Celia explained about the nursery business, and made it the excuse for her call. "This is a sordid commercial enquiry and I feel bad about involving you, but you must know everyone in your bit of Oxfordshire. Does the name Martens mean anything to you?"

"Of course. The Martens are Alastair Rendle's in-laws. Alastair and Elsa are bosom pals of ours. We were over at Baddeley the other day."

"I see," said Celia, fascinated. "Could you tell me a bit about them?"

"Of course, let me bring you up to date with what goes on at Baddeley. Alastair's taken over there now, was in the navy, he's the great-nephew. The old lady died last year, she was nearly a hundred, and of course the bill for death duties is phenomenal and Alastair and Elsa can't pay it, and the National Trust won't help them out because they can't produce an endowment. They've put a brave face on it, opened the house to the public and so on, but of course that won't bring in enough to pay the death duties. We're all desperately sorry for them, but what can one do?"

"You say Elsa Rendle's maiden name was Martens?" Celia asked.

"That's right. Her father was Dutch, killed in the war but her mother's English and the children were brought up here."

"Does her mother live in England?" Celia asked.

"Yes, in King's Easton to be near Elsa, who's a sweetie. She and Alastair are blissfully happy together and there are two boys in their twenties, both charmers, one of them in the army and the other in the Fleet Air Arm. But I'm gossiping, what did you want to know?"

"I wondered if Elsa had a brother."

"Yes, he's an art dealer in Amsterdam, doing very well, I believe."

"A big man, with rimless glasses and a gingery beard?"

"No, it can't be the same chap. Our Martens is clean-shaven and doesn't wear glasses. He's a bachelor, very civilized. Comes over a lot to see his mother and sister, and is much in demand as a spare man."

"Oh, then he can't be the Martens who owes me six hundred pounds for species rhododendrons," she fibbed. "I'm glad it isn't, the family sounds rather nice."

They chatted on for a little longer, but Celia's mind was furiously busy. The owner of Baddeley Court was faced with a huge bill for death duties, and had no means of paying it. He had two sons described as charmers, who were probably strapping enough to help him carry a heavy piece of sculpture. All three men had service backgrounds which fitted them temperamentally for adventure, and one of them was in the Fleet Air Arm, which probably meant experience with helicopters. The brother-in-law was called Martens and was clean-shaven. But his pose as Nigel Monk called for some sort of disguise. A pair of not too strong glasses were easily acquired, and it was equally easy to grow a beard.

Filled with zest for the chase, Celia reached for the guide to stately homes open to the public. Baddeley court near Bicester, the home of Captain Alastair Rendle, RN, was open daily except Tuesdays, and the next step was obvious.

❧ NINE ❧

Baddeley Court proved to be in an imposing Georgian mansion standing in a neglected park. Celia paid a stiff entrance fee and bought a guidebook. The introduction gave the history of the family, ending with the story of "the present owner's great-aunt who survived her husband by fifty years and her only son by forty, and lived on in the mansion, alone but for two elderly servants, becoming more and more of a recluse, till she herself died at the age of ninety-eight."

A route had been marked out with arrows, to direct visitors round the house. There were few of them, for it was not a major tourist attraction. The rooms were handsome, but they were furnished with a curious mixture of gracious Georgian and gimcrack Edwardian. The pictures were family portraits of no great distinction, mixed up with feeble amateur water-colors. Compared with most other stately homes, with village ladies in attendance and bowls of flowers in every room, the whole place was amateur.

Tiger skins with great stuffed heads snarling up from the floor bore witness to Victorian big-game shoots in India. Where was the gunroom? There had to be one in this sort of house, but it was probably tucked away in the private quarters, and police regulations would certainly require it to be securely locked. Sporting guns had been used in the operation at the Villa Salvadori. Had they been put back in their racks in the gunroom at Baddeley after use? Perhaps, and no doubt they were properly registered with the police.

Why had she come here? Celia wondered. She had not expected to find the stolen treasure from the Villa Salvadori on public show, and the only sculptures to be seen were sentimental Victorian busts of children. Having investigated Edwardian sleeping and bathing arrangements upstairs, she followed the arrowed route of the tour down into the basement, which the guidebook stressed as a major attraction; the unaltered domestic offices of a Georgian household. The arrows directed her into a vast, barbaric kitchen, and beyond it through echoing still-rooms, cellars and sculleries. And in an alcove in one of them she came upon a small marble statue.

No, she decided, this can't be it. It was only about four feet high, too small and unimportant looking. If it was the stolen treasure from Italy, surely it ought to be hidden away under lock and key? But if it was a family heirloom handed down from generation to generation, what was it doing in disgrace down in the basement and not in an honoured place upstairs?

It represented a handsome young man, but with goatish horns growing out of his forehead, and pointed animal-like ears. He was leaning against the trunk of a tree, naked except for what looked like an animal skin draped round his shoulders, with a set of pan-pipes in his right hand. His youthful figure was soft and effeminate, and his head was thrown back. His lips were slightly open in a very sexy smile. He was beautiful, but could he be the loot from Italy?

She went back to the front hall. The woman who had sold her a ticket and guidebook had been replaced by a man in his late forties with the genial but self-assured look which went with service in the navy.

"Captain Rendle?" she inquired.

"Yes, my dear. What can I do for you?"

"I wonder if you can tell me anything about the sculpture down in the cellars? The guidebook doesn't mention it."

"Ah, there's quite a story about that. We meant to put it in the guide but we forgot. My great-great-great-grandfather won it in a wager. Someone bet him he couldn't ride his horse up the main staircase of a house in London, but he did."

"Goodness. It can't have been a very steep staircase."

"Probably not. The house belonged to a chap called Lord Camelford, he and my great-great-great-grandfather were pretty wild lads. Anyway, my distinguished ancestor won his bet, and Camelford had to hand over the statue."

"So it's been in the family a long time," said Celia.

"Yes, since about the end of the eighteenth century."

"Standing down there in the cellar?"

"The Victorian Rendles decided it was rude, and put it down there. My great-aunt didn't fancy it either, in fact everyone had forgotten about it till my wife and I went exploring the cellars and turned out a huge accumulation of rubbish. Quite a jolly bit of eighteenth-century nonsense don't you think? When we've got the energy we'll clean it up a bit and have it brought upstairs."

Celia left, with every nerve tingling. So the statue had allegedly been in the cellar for at least a hundred and fifty years. Within living memory the house had been occupied by an elderly recluse, living alone with two doddery old servants who had probably not ventured into the rubbish-choked cellars for years and had only the vaguest idea of what they did or did not contain. It was a perfect set-up. Quite soon some connoisseur visiting the house would spot the neglected sculpture in the cellar and tell the Rendles that it was not a jolly bit of eighteenth-century nonsense. They would make a convincing show of being astonished and delighted to learn of its true value. Because of the export restrictions they could not expect to sell it for what it would fetch on the open market, but it would clear the death duties on the Baddeley estate. Moreover it would be accepted at once as genuine. As a legend to account for its appearance

174

from nowhere, the fable about Lord Camelford, the horse and the cellar was infinitely more credible than the middle of the Adriatic or a private collection in Switzerland.

But on the way back to Archerscroft, doubts set in. Lord Camelford, whoever he was, encouraged people to ride horses up his staircase. If the Rendles were trying to invent respectable origins for a stolen antique, why had they imported such a disorderly person into its pedigree? Research was called for. Once again, she had to return home via the reference section of the public library.

Thomas Pitt, first Baron Camelford, she read in the *Dictionary of National Biography*. He had been born in 1737 and died in 1793 in Italy. From March 1762 he had lived in Twickenham, where he jokingly called his house the Palazzo Pitti and was a neighbour of Horace Walpole, who regarded him as an authority on architecture. Later, he had built himself Camelford House, in Oxford Street at the top of Park Lane, an area which has long since become a wilderness of multiple stores. He was also a member of something called the Society of Dilettanti, but what was that? An encyclopedia enlightened her. According to a contemporary document:

> "In the year 1734 some gentlemen who had travelled in Italy, desirous of encouraging at home a taste for those objects which had contributed so much to their entertainment abroad, formed themselves into a Society under the name of *The Dilettanti*, and agreed upon such resolutions as they thought necessary to keep up the spirit of the scheme."*

Reading on, Celia discovered that the objects found entertaining in Italy by the Dilettanti were antique statues, inscriptions, coins and gems. Importing such relics of the ancient world had been all the rage among Englishmen of

---

*But Horace Walpole, writing a letter on 14th April 1743, gives a different picture of the Dilettanti as "a club, for which the nominal qualification is having been in Italy, and the real one, being drunk; the two chiefs are Lord Middlesex and Sir Francis Dashwood, who were seldom sober the whole time they were in Italy."

taste throughout the eighteenth century, and a brisk trade had grown up in fakes manufactured with the British market in mind. Horace Walpole, Camelford's neighbour at Twickenham, had been a leading member of the Dilettanti, and if the Rendles chose to allege that Camelford had possessed a valuable Greek or Roman statue, it would take a brave expert on these matters to deny it.

On the other hand, Camelford had taken himself seriously as a politician as well as a connoisseur of the antique. There was no hint in his cv of wild behaviour and horses being ridden upstairs. What about the next generation? She returned to the *Dictionary of National Biography*.

Thomas Pitt, second Baron Camelford, had been born in 1775, educated partly in Switzerland (why?) and in 1789 sent into the navy, which his father perhaps regarded as a suitable receptacle for an unsatisfactory son. Despite feats of good seamanship and bravery, he kept being discharged in disgrace for "acts of insubordination", and on one occasion was put on shore in Malacca to find his own way home to England. In the West Indies he had shot a fellow-officer dead in a quarrel over seniority in which he was in the wrong, but managed to convince a court-martial that he had been quelling a mutiny. Back in London as the second Lord Camelford, he refused to light up Camelford House during the celebrations of the peace with France of 1801, and had all the windows broken by the mob as a result. On another occasion passers-by in the street had to restrain him from caning a man who refused to meet him in a duel on the grounds that he had given no offence, and he had been fined £500 for throwing a Mr. Humphries downstairs in a quarrel at the theatre. He had been killed in a duel in 1804, and left to moulder in his coffin in a church in Soho because a fresh outbreak of the war with France had made his wish to be buried in Switzerland impossible to fulfill.

As he left no issue, the title became extinct, and there was no repository of family papers for researchers to ferret into and raise awkward questions. A man capable of throwing fellow theatre-goers down staircases was obviously capable of encouraging his friends to ride horses up them, and Celia was forced to conclude that the Rendles had produced a well-researched certificate of respectability for their stolen treasure.

She went home, and composed a long letter to Commissario Ciampi, detailing her discoveries. Knowing how much he disliked detection by anyone but himself, let alone a foreign female who was supposed to be minding her own business, she tried to soften the blow. "It may be that what I have stumbled across is just a series of coincidences, but I thought I should bring them to your attention. I know you think it unlikely for a stolen work of major importance to be brought to Britain for disposal because the difficulty over the export license would depress the price. That consideration might well deter professional thieves, but amateurs with no experience of selling a stolen work with a dubious provenance are in a different position. I wonder if the Rendles may not have been attracted by the idea of giving their prize a fictitious English pedigree which will be difficult to disprove, and settling for a lesser sum, which is all they need to clear a crippling debt for death duties."

Ciampi would take the next paragraph badly, because he ought to have checked the point as a matter of routine, but that could not be helped. "I seem to remember," she concluded, "that you have prints of the holiday pictures taken by the people on our tour, and that a tall man with glasses and a gingery beard appears in some of them. He was travelling as Nigel Monk, but have you compared these pictures with any you have of Nicolaes Martens in his normal appearance? It seems clear that they represent the same person."

Judge Merlini leafed through the collection of photographs which Ciampi had handed him, and put them down on his desk. "It is a pity, Alessandro, that you did not notice this resemblance earlier. You sometimes show a deplorable lack of imagination."

Ciampi managed somehow to keep his fury to himself. "It did not occur to me, any more than it did to you, that Martens might have joined the tour under an assumed name."

"Where is Martens at present?"

"Still in Amsterdam, I think. He gave the Dutch police a detailed account, which we have checked, of the legitimate business negotiations which brought him to Lucca, and he denies ever having visited the Villa Salvadori."

"He must be questioned again. Arrange it with the Dutch."

"I think also that I should go to England to examine this statue," said Ciampi.

"Why? As a dramatic move to impress the journalists? No. You are not an expert on ancient marbles. Send Petroni. There is still no trace of the Vincents?"

"None. The British police think they may be in Spain, but we have found no trace of them there."

"It astonishes me that you still refuse to issue their pictures and description to the media."

"You know my reasons. Their handicapped child is still in a hospice in England. The British police have undertaken to take them in for questioning when they call to collect him. They will not dare to do so if they know that they have been identified with the Hansons and that every police force in Europe has been asked to look for them."

"But two months have passed, and the child is still there."

"Mrs. Vincent is devoted to him and will not accept a permanent separation. They will certainly return, provided they think it safe."

"And meanwhile, the media make us look foolish."

"That cannot be helped."

* * *

"This is a very interesting piece, Captain Rendle," said the expert from the Ashmolean Museum in Oxford.

"Yes. Quite a jolly bit of eighteenth-century nonsense, don't you think?"

The expert did not comment, but examined the statue's backside. "Do you know how it came to be at Baddeley?"

"There's a family tradition that one of my raffish ancestors won it for a bet," said Alastair.

"Really? Does the family tradition say who he won it from?"

Alastair rattled off the fable about Lord Camelford, the horse and the staircase which his brother-in-law Nick Martens had worked out for him, and made a show of polite interest when he was told that the first Lord Camelford had been a member of the Dilettanti and a well-known collector of ancient statuary.

"His son was very wild, I seem to remember?" said the expert. "There were a lot of scandals about him. It's quite possible that he disposed of an important work in the manner you describe."

He examined the statue again in great detail, peering at every inch of the surface.

"A colleague of mine from another museum happened to come round your house last week," he went on. "His suspicions were aroused when he saw it, and they were correct."

"Suspicions?" Alastair asked. "You mean, it's a fake?"

"Certainly not, the work is definitely ancient. No eighteenth-century sculptor would have access to Pentelic marble, and the tradition connecting it with the Camelford collection gives it an impeccable provenance. On stylistic grounds I would say that it dates from the fourth century B.C. and is an early copy of a Praxitelean original."

"I suppose that makes it worth a bit more than we thought?" said Alastair.

"We live in crazy times, Captain Rendle. Prices in the

179

sale-room have gone through the roof. On the open market, you could reckon on five million pounds at least."

Alastair made strenuous efforts to look surprised. "Good Lord. And I don't think I can afford to insure it."

He was delighted that the whole thing had gone so smoothly. It had started in a casual after-dinner conversation over the brandy and cigars, when his brother-in-law Nick Martens mentioned to him that one of his contacts in the shady art world knew of an antique statue being offered for illicit sale at a monstrous price. Nick had jokingly sketched out a scenario for stealing it to pay off the death duties on Baddeley Court. Alastair could not remember when he realised that as far as Nick was concerned, it was not a daydream, but a plan for action, carefully worked out down to the last detail. His first reaction was to tell Nick he was mad. But Nick pointed out that this was a once-in-a-lifetime chance, the only way of saving Baddeley from the auctioneers. So Alastair talked to his two boys about it and Nick talked to them too, and they were keen, and Nick explained how nothing could go wrong.

Nick was right about that. Nothing had.

Maidstone was Jane Armstrong's shopping town, and she had not forgotten that Tom Vincent was an inmate of the hospice near the station. She had looked in there for an hour, and been touched by what she found. Her well-developed social conscience told her that one ought to give time to the handicapped, and the mother superior had welcomed her offer to come again. That was a month ago, and she had been coming to see Tom Vincent several times a week.

She had struck up a firm friendship with Tom. As soon as she arrived in the room where the children spent the day, he would run up to her grinning broadly and show her drawings he had made or search her pockets for the small presents she brought him. This time it was a simple jigsaw puzzle, too large to go in a pocket. But he enjoyed searching for things and finding them, so she had put it under her cardigan in a plastic carrier bag.

Tom took his time finding it, then started fitting the puzzle together, appealing to Jane for help when a difficulty made him frustrated and angry. After he had done it three times, he had mastered it and was bored. So she took him and some of the others out into the garden and played round games with them till it was time for their tea. Having helped serve it, she left to go home.

And on her way out through the front hall of the hospice she came astonishingly face to face with Tom's parents, on their way in.

Both parties stood stock still, as they realised the implications of this encounter.

"Why, it's you, Jane," said Paula Vincent. "What are you doing here?"

Instinct warned Jane that the truth was too embarrassing to be told. "I . . . just happened to look in to see a friend of mine on the staff," she managed.

The mother superior came out of her office, caught sight of the Vincents and looked disconcerted.

"Hullo, Reverend Mother," said Paula. "Sorry about the short notice, but we've come to take Tom away."

"Ah, Mrs. Vincent." For some reason, the mother superior seemed to be as embarrassed as Jane was. "I'll . . . give instructions for Tom to be got ready. Meanwhile, I'm so glad you've met up with Jane here. She's been wonderful while you've been away. You'll see a great improvement in Tom, she's been visiting him almost daily and she's brought him on a lot."

"Has she indeed?" said Jimmy with a death's-head grin.

"Oh yes, you'll notice the difference at once. Will you excuse me a moment while I make an urgent phone call?"

Jimmy waited till she had gone, then said: "Let's get into the car, Jane, and have a little talk."

Panic seized Jane. "I can't, I'm afraid, I'm in rather a hurry."

"It won't take a moment."

"But I don't want to," she said, and hurried out of the building.

He followed her and gripped her arm. "To hell with what you want, get in the car."

"No!"

He was sticking something into the back of her sweater. "If you scream or make a fuss you'll get this between your ribs."

A Ford Fiesta was parked in the driveway. He marched her towards it.

"Jimmy, for God's sake," Paula protested.

"Open the door," he gasped.

"But Jimmy—"

"Do as you're told, damn your eyes."

He bundled Jane into the back of the car, pushed Paula into the front passenger seat, got in himself and drove off.

"You must be mad, why did you do that?" Paula asked as the car gathered speed.

"You'll find out."

"And now we've got her, what the hell do we do with her?"

"We try to keep quiet," he said in steely tones, "and not drive each other mad if we can help it. And presently we will find a quiet spot where we can stop the car and talk."

"Fine, we'll have someone with you at once to question them," said the desk sergeant at Maidstone police station when the convent reported that the Vincents had arrived to collect their child. The mother superior was surprised, on returning to the front hall, to find it empty, but assumed that the Vincents had gone into the ward to see their son. The squad car arrived and took some minutes to establish that the Vincents were nowhere in the building. After more delay one of the novices volunteered that she had been looking out of a window and saw them drive away hastily in a car which she could only describe as smallish and red. Jane Armstrong was with them, and they seemed to be cross with her for some reason.

In the Ford Fiesta, Jane was inwardly cursing for letting herself be conned so easily. Jimmy had forced her into the car not with a knife or gun but with a ball-point pen at her back, she had seen it clearly for a moment as he pushed her into the rear seat. She was trapped, the car had only two doors, and access to them was blocked by the seats in front of her and their hefty occupants. But if their only weapon was a ball-point pen, all was not lost. With all the windows shut there was little point in shouting for help, but there were other ways of attracting attention.

In the centre of the town the car had to stop in a long tailback at some traffic-lights, with people on the pavement coming in and out of shops. She had written "Am being abducted, call police" on a scrap of paper from her bag, and held it up against the nearside window with an agonized expression on her face. But the shoppers did not notice or looked away, anxious not to become involved.

Presently Jimmy Vincent noticed what she was doing. He swung round in his seat and slapped her hard across the face. "Stop that or I'll break your neck."

Jane decided that if he wanted a fight, he could have one and attacked his face, with her fingernails. They struggled. The traffic-lights had gone green, and cars behind the stationary Fiesta were hooting. Paula joined in the fight, and pinned Jane against the back seat with her fingers round her throat.

With order more or less restored, Jimmy drove on across the traffic-lights. But an elderly man who had witnessed the scene from the pavement decided, after some hesitation, to ring the police and tell them he had seen a girl in a red Fiesta, registration number such-and-such, hold up a note to the window and try to attract the attention of passers-by, after which she had been violently attacked by the people in the front seats.

Clear of the town, Jimmy turned off the main road into a network of lonely lanes on the slope of the North Downs. A small roadside wood concealed a disused, ivy-grown chalk pit. He drove the car into it, made Paula give him her scarf, and used it to tie Jane's wrists together behind her. After dealing similarly with her ankles, using his own necktie, he rummaged in the boot of the car and brought out the heavy handle of the jack.

"Any funny business and you get this over the head," he told her.

"Fine, so what happens next?" Paula asked sourly.

"We find out how much this wretched girl knows, and how she comes to know it."

Four days had passed, and Celia had heard nothing from Ciampi. But on the evening of the fifth, she had a call from Dr. Petroni. "Commissario Ciampi has received your letter," he said, "and we decided that the first step was for me to examine the statue which you have so cleverly found. I thought you would be interested to know that I have come to England for this purpose."

"I am indeed interested. Do you think the Baddeley statue could be the missing work from the Villa Salvadori?"

"It is possible, but one important detail you have omitted from your description. Was it equipped with a tail?"

"A tail. You mean, like an animal's?"

"A short curling tail like that of a goat, rising from the buttocks."

"I don't know, I didn't look at its back. One doesn't expect boys to have tails. Is it important?"

"Yes. A week ago Ciampi broke down the resistance of Enrico Fabbri, the youngest of the Salvadori gardeners, and made him describe the statue found in the underground passage. It is clear that it represented a satyr, a frequent motif in Graceo–Roman art, as also did the one you saw. A tail is sometimes present, but not always, and according to young Fabbri the Salvadori example possessed this appendage. I shall be interested to see if it is present in the one at Baddeley Court.''

"So would I, Dr. Petroni. Where are you phoning from?''

"A hotel near Gatwick airport. Very noisy.''

"I'm only fifteen miles from you. Would you like me to pick you up tomorrow morning and drive you over to Oxfordshire? You'd have a tiresome cross-country journey if you went by train, and Baddeley's miles from the nearest station.''

"How kind. I accept with great pleasure, and will be delighted to go there in your company. May I add that I am filled with admiration for what you have achieved, and I think I can say the same for Commissario Ciampi. As you may have observed, he does not always welcome suggestions made to him, but in this case even he finds himself making an exception.''

It was almost dark, and the Vincents had not moved on from the chalk pit. Jane, trussed up in the back seat, was very uncomfortable but less terrified than she had expected to be, for her position was stronger than she had thought. She had pointed out to the Vincents that she was not the only person who knew of their masquerade as the Hansons, since Celia had recognized them at once and told the police. Therefore, she argued, the Vincents would do themselves no good by silencing her, and they might as well let her go.

But the Vincents took no notice. Jimmy had found a local station on the car radio, and they had listened to the news. The nuns had raised the alarm, the police knew that Jane had been taken hostage, they had even discovered the number of the car. Anyone who saw it was asked to contact the nearest police station immediately. Since hearing that, the Vincents had spent their time working themselves up into an ever-increasing panic and quarreling with each other.

"It was you insisted on coming back for Tom," snarled

Jimmy. "Safe as houses, you said. And look where it's got us."

"You promised me we would," she wailed. "You did, right at the beginning. I only agreed to that mad business because we needed the money for Tom."

"Well, I came back, didn't I?"

"Only because I had the money tied up so that you can't go off on your own and spend it. Even then I had to nag you for weeks before you agreed. You've never loved Tom, you meant to leave him here till he died while we enjoyed ourselves on the Costa Brava."

"Listen, let's be practical. We're thirty miles from Dover, there's a ferry to Calais every hour. Let's get out while we can."

"No!" Paula shouted. "I'm not leaving England again without Tom."

For the second time since they had stopped in the chalk pit, Paula got out of the car and walked off down the lane, saying that Jimmy could do what he liked, she was damned if she'd desert her son. Each time he simply sat in the car and waited for her to come back. If she went back to the hospice she would be arrested at once, and she knew it.

Raucous music on the car radio was faded down for another newscast. It repeated the information from the previous one and added that the Vincents were wanted for questioning in connection with a crime committed in Italy.

"You hear?" screamed Paula. "And you want us to go to the ferry terminal and try to go through the passport control with two passports in the name of Vincent. There's nothing we can do, we're trapped."

Jimmy was concentrating on another problem. "We'll have to get rid of the car."

"So what do we do without it?" Paula demanded. "Walk, dragging our hostage along behind us on the end of a rope?"

"Shut up, Paula, you bitch."

Jane was really frightened now. They had nothing to gain

by silencing her. But in their present state of hysteria, they were quite capable of killing her out of sheer bad temper. It would be wise to try to calm them down.

"Aren't you making rather heavy weather over this?" she asked. "What you did in Italy isn't so very terrible. You were involved in a conspiracy to steal, but you weren't a party to the Prices' murder. Why don't you give yourselves up? I won't bring a charge against you, and after you've done a year or two in prison you can collect Tom and live on the money you got for pretending to be kidnapped."

"She's right, you know," said Paula. "It's the only way out of this mess."

Jimmy started the engine. "I'm not serving a prison sentence for the sake of your deformed brat," he said, and backed out of the chalk pit.

"Where are we going?" Paula asked.

"To find a phone box. I've had an idea."

"What sort of an idea?" Paula asked crossly.

"Tell you when we get there."

He found a phone by a deserted crossroads in a fold of the downs. Paula got out of the car for a moment and they conferred in low tones beside it.

"You can try, it might work," said Paula doubtfully, and climbed in again.

In the phone box, Jimmy rang Nick Martens' number in Amsterdam.

"What the hell d'you mean, ringing me at this hour?" Martens grumbled sleepily.

"Disaster. We're in the shit up to our necks. We were wrong about the Grant woman."

"What d'you mean? Talk sense, can't you?"

"She recognized Paula and me from the first go and kept quiet about it."

"So?"

"So she told the police, and they're on to us."

"Where are you?"

"In a call box in the wilds of Kent."

"What the hell are you doing there? You're supposed to be in Spain."

"Paula insisted on coming back for the child."

"Well, you can get back to Spain pronto."

"We can't. The police will be watching the ports for us."

"That's your problem."

"Not entirely. If we get in a mess, you'll be in a worse one."

"You mean, you'll tell the whole story?"

"What else could we do?"

There was a pause while this disagreeable news sank in. "So what am I supposed to do about it?" Martens asked.

"You can find us somewhere to lay up till you can get us false passports."

"Can I hell. They don't grow on trees. You two are a pair of squalid nuisances."

"I daresay, but you'll have to do something about us quick."

Martens thought intensively, and hit on a course of action. "OK then, you win. I know a place where you can lie up while we dope something out."

"Fine, but how do we get there? The police have even got the number of our car."

"Hell, you don't do things by halves, do you? Listen, there's a car ferry from Calais that gets into Dover about eight in the morning. I'll be on it. Wait for me at the filling station by the Eastern Docks exit—"

"No. Too near the ferry terminal. The police'll be watching for us."

"Outside the White Cliffs Hotel then, and I'll drive you to the cottage."

Back at the car, he murmured "that's fixed" to Paula and drove off. To frustrate police cars on the lookout for the Fiesta he had taken the bulb out of the light over the rear number plate. As an additional precaution he took a route to the coast through quiet, unfrequented lanes, stopping at intervals in lay-bys and turning out the lights while he and Paula smoked cigarettes and even, incredibly, slept a little. They were filling in time, Jane decided, but why?

An hour before dawn he drove on to the coast, and parked at a lonely spot near the monument high on the cliffs above the English Channel, which commemorates the dead of the Dover Patrol during the First World War.

"Help me get her out of the car," he told Paula.

"Why? What d'you mean?"

"What d'you think I mean?"

"Jimmy, I won't be a party to murder," Paula screamed. "If you do it, you'll be on your own. I shall stay here till the morning, and tell the police what you've done."

"Don't be so bloody idiotic. Help me to get her out."

"If you're proposing to push me over the cliff, you'd better think again," Jane interrupted. "There's no point in it and you'll get life sentences instead of a year or two."

He took no notice, and dragged her out of the car by her feet. Laying her on the grass, he checked that she was trussed up tight, then gagged her with his handkerchief and pulled her into some scrubby bushes.

"We'll be well away before she's found," he told Paula as they drove off. "Thought I'd really do it, didn't you? She was quite right, there was no point. But she deserved a good fright, the silly little bitch."

As the car gathered speed he burst into hysterical laughter. But Paula did not join in.

❧ TEN ❧

Something blessedly warm was wetting Jane's cheek. She opened her eyes, and found herself being licked by a mongrel dog. Her hands were still tied behind her back and her legs fastened together at the ankles. She had struggled to free herself for a time, but failed and had been lying for hours in the dew-drenched grass. She was chilled to the marrow and very stiff.

The dog's owner, out for an early morning walk, proved efficient as well as sympathetic. He half carried her back to his bungalow above St. Margaret's Bay, caused his wife to ply her with hot-water bottles and scalding coffee, and telephoned her parents, the hospice and the police.

Presently her teeth stopped chattering and she was able to start on an enormous breakfast. The police arrived and reported that the Ford Fiesta had been found abandoned in a back street in Dover. "But they can't have taken the ferry, Miss. Passport control were watching out for them."

"Just before midnight Mr. Vincent said he'd thought of a plan, and telephoned someone," Jane remembered. "And I think the other person must have said OK, because he was a lot calmer after that."

"You don't know who he phoned, Miss?"

"No." After two more mouthfuls of bacon and egg, she added: "Actually, there's someone who knows much more than I do about all this. She might be able to help you. Would you like me to ring her?"

"Please, Miss."

As she hoped, Celia had a suggestion, but it was very tentative. "There are two places in England where they might have gone into hiding, both of them in Oxfordshire. This is a long shot, and I don't guarantee anything. But if you put your policeman on the line I'll give him the details."

Jane's phone call had caught Celia just before she left to pick up Dr. Petroni at his hotel and drive him to Baddeley Court. She was unnerved at herself for having suggested even tentatively to the police that the Vincents might have gone to ground either there or at the cottage belonging to Nicolaes Martens' mother. What if she arrived at Baddeley to find police ransacking the place in vain and having to apologize to Captain Rendle because the Vincents were not there?

Baddeley was indeed under siege when she and Petroni reached it, but only by curious sightseers and the media. The news that an expert had pronounced the Baddeley satyr ancient had been published in the morning papers. A flock of journalists and television crews was crowding round it, and Alastair Rendle was telling the story of Lord Camelford, the horse and the staircase to a succession of radio and TV interviewers. Some time passed before Dr. Petroni could get near enough to the statue to examine it properly. Having done so he withdrew into Celia's car to report to her.

"Well, what did you make of it?" she asked.

"The motif of a resting satyr is a very familiar one. A great many similar figures were made in Graeco–Roman times to decorate villas and gardens. But this example is quite outstanding, and cannot be later in date than the fourth century B.C., which means that it is very closely related to the lost original by Praxiteles from which so many other examples were derived."

"So it is the sort of thing that would be well worth stealing."

"Indeed yes, and it is in excellent condition. The body was carved separately from the head, but is clearly the original one, both are in the same Pentelic marble. The right arm holding the syrinx and the lower edge of the nebris, or fawn-skin, are additions by a restorer. The left arm is original, but has been broken and replaced at the wrong angle. It must once have held a spear or shepherd's crook, as a fragment of its shaft is attached to the base. In the eighteenth century it was obligatory to 'restore' incomplete classical statues, and the additions were often carried out in an arbitrary and tasteless manner. But for reasons of style I am convinced that in this case the work was carried out by Bartolommeo Cavaceppi, one of the least incompetent of the sculptors engaged in this sad work."

"What sort of money are we talking about?" Celia asked.

Petroni opened his arms wide. "This is a work of real quality. On the open market we are envisaging ten million dollars at least."

"And what about Captain Rendle's account of how it came into the family? Is it believable?"

"Unfortunately he has devised a story which will be difficult to disprove. Michaelis,* the Mid-Victorian authority on classical sculptures in Britain makes no mention of this work. But as he admits, there were many sculptures in private collections of which he had no knowledge, moreover Lord Camelford's collection had been dispersed long before Michaelis composed his monumental volume. But the first Lord Camelford is mentioned very briefly in an unreliable, rather gossipy book written at the beginning of the nineteenth century by a clergyman who saw some of the more famous collections and wrote from hearsay about others.† He says only: 'a fountain nymph and several other

---

*A. T. F. Michaelis, *Ancient Marbles in Great Britain*. London 1861.
†The Rev. James Dallaway, *Anecdotes of the Arts*. London 1800.

good statues were collected by the late Lord Camelford'. This provides the Baddeley Court statue with the authority of an almost-contemporary witness, but is vague enough to admit the possibility that Lord Camelford possessed not only a nymph but also, among other works, a satyr of the first quality, which was transferred to the Baddeley family under the disreputable circumstances which you have described.''

"I wonder if one could prove that the staircase at Camelford House was the sort you couldn't get a horse up,'' Celia mused. "Otherwise the only way out is to discover where the thing really came from.''

"We know already its true provenance. You see, Signora, the restorer I have mentioned, Bartolommeo Cavaceppi published a *Raccolta d'Antiche Statue*, listing all the statues which passed through his hands, and one of the many satyrs was sold to the Mansis, a rich family of Lucca. At that time they were leaving their magnificent palazzo in the centre of Lucca, and establishing themselves in the country at the Villa Mansi, which I believe you visited during your tour.''

"That's right!'' said Celia. "That was one of the places with a bed that Napoleon had slept in.''

"*Appunto*! Foreseeing that such an event might take place, and knowing that the Emperor frequently removed important works of art to Paris, the Mansis decided to take precautions concerning a possession of theirs which might have tempted him. I need only add that the villa of their friends and neighbors the Salvadoris is to be found only ten kilometres away.''

"And that clinches it,'' said Celia. "You can tell the police who the real owner is, and say all this talk about horses and staircases is a load of poppycock.''

"Unfortunately, no. Cavaceppi's records show that he also sold several satyrs for export to England, without always noting who the purchaser was. So if I say 'Mansi' and the Capitano Rendle says 'Camelford', who is to decide which is telling a lie?''

"So what happens now?'' Celia asked.

"I return to Italy and report."

"I see. But there are sandwiches and a bottle of quite nice wine in the car. Why don't we go out into the park and enjoy those first?"

"Hell no, Nick," said Alastair Rendle. "We can't have those two here."

Martens' Jaguar had swept into the stable-yard at Baddeley just before noon. The Vincents were still sitting in it. Alastair glared at them. "What's wrong with digs, or some quiet private hotel?"

"According to Vincent, his wife wants to give herself up and face the consequences, which would be bearable for her and very serious for us. Unless we keep an eye on them, she'll be off in a flash, confessing to the local constabulary."

"So?"

"She's got to be locked up somewhere, and the only place I could think of is your attic."

"No. She'd make a row and the public would hear."

"Not if Vincent is with her and they're told they've been locked in for their own safety. Come on, Alastair, the sooner they're out of sight the better."

"You realize we've got hordes of people here gaping at the statue? Plus the media in force?"

Nick made a disgusted face. "Chosen the wrong moment to go public with it, haven't you?"

"How was I to know you'd choose today to lumber me with those two and tell me the whole damn thing's come unstuck?"

"It hasn't come unstuck yet, not if we keep our heads. The Grant woman recognized the Vincents, but she doesn't know my real name and she can't have made the connection between you and the Villa Salvadori. For God's sake, Alastair, don't stand there like a moonstruck rabbit. Does the door at the bottom of your attic staircase lock?"

"I think so, yes."

"Come on then, what are we waiting for?"

The attic at Baddeley was a rabbit-warren of long-disused servants' bedrooms, cramped and sordid. The Vincents were smuggled into it up a back staircase and the door locked on the outside.

"We'll come back soon as we can to make you more comfortable," Alastair told them.

On the way downstairs Nick paused and gripped Alastair's arm. "Those two know too much. You'll have to do something drastic about them."

"What the hell d'you mean?"

"What d'you think I mean?"

Alastair looked at him uneasily. "Why me? Why not you?"

"I haven't got a son with a murder rap hanging over him."

"Poor kid, he lost his head."

"You should keep your children under better control. Killing the Prices was quite unnecessary, all you had to do was to make sure they didn't see you carry the damn statue into the helicopter."

For a few moments Alastair gazed out of the staircase window, deep in thought. "Nick, why did you bring the Vincents here?"

"I've told you."

"That's not the real reason. I've been thinking. You've been the brains behind this whole thing, but you fixed it so that we took all the risks."

"And took all the profits, apart from my ten per cent," Nick reminded him.

"But when the Vincents came unstuck, you realized that if they were arrested and talked, you'd be the one they talked about, because they didn't know about me. That's why you brought them to Baddeley. They know about me now. You've engineered it so that I have an even stronger motive than you have for rubbing them out, and now you want to leave the dirty work to me. I'm not having that, Nick. I draw the line at cold-blooded murder."

"If you prefer to let that boy of yours stand trial in Italy for killing the Prices, that's your affair."

"My God, I was mad to let you talk me into this. Let's think, there must be some other way. How about offering them a lot more money?"

Left alone in the dusty attic, the Vincents reviewed their situation.

"Who was that other man with Martens?" Paula asked.

"The owner of the house, I suppose."

"And the ringleader of the helicopter crew?"

"Could be," said Jimmy. "We never saw their faces."

Paula went down the short flight of attic stairs and tested the door. "Why did they lock it on the outside, instead of giving us the key?"

"No idea. Does it matter?"

After thinking about this, Paula said: "Jimmy, you didn't tell Martens that I wanted to tell the whole story to the police?"

"No, of course not."

After all these years, she could tell when he was lying. Suddenly she was rigid with anger. "You did! You told him when you and Martens got out to pee into the hedge. That's why they've locked the door on the outside. They're afraid I'll escape."

"Oh shut up, Paula. You're imagining things."

"No I'm not. Hasn't it occurred to you that there's another murder in the pipeline, with us as the victims? We know the whole story now, including the fact that this house is somehow involved. Thanks to your idiocy, they know that I want to come clean and get the whole thing off our backs. We're an embarrassment to them as long as we're alive. Nobody but them knows we're here and there's a huge park to bury us in. I'm terrified, Jimmy, and so would you be if you had any sense."

"Stop it, Paula, you're driving me mad."

"You're so stupid. When anything bad comes along, you bury your head in the sand and pretend it hasn't happened."

In a flash they were off again, arguing over the well-trodden battleground. She was responsible for everything that had gone wrong with their lives, he complained, for their failed careers in the theatre, for the handicapped child, for the fix they were in because she insisted on coming back for him. Paula retorted that he had never cared for Tom, had intended to let him rot in the hospice till he died. She had always been against the Italian business, he had talked her into it. Why had he lost his head and kidnapped Jane Armstrong?

She was shouting. Jimmy put a hand over her mouth to quieten her. He was white with rage, furious with her for being right: they were caught in a trap, and would never get out alive.

The Vincents were out of sight, but Martens' Jaguar was not, and an alert detective constable, sent to Baddeley in case Celia's tip-off proved correct, had seen it arrive and noted its number. As a result of the report he made, two large police cars arrived as Celia and Dr. Petroni returned to the carpark after their picnic. Instead of driving away, they stayed to gape unashamedly and await developments. The television crews and the sightseers attracted by the satyr did likewise.

"Captain Rendle?" said the inspector in charge. "I have reason to believe that two people are in this house whom we wish to interview in connection with the kidnapping of a young woman yesterday in Kent."

"Oh, why should you think that?" said Alastair, choking down inward panic.

"They were observed by the hall porter of the White Cliffs Hotel in Dover, loitering and acting suspiciously on the pavement outside. They were there for over an hour, obviously waiting for somebody who had been delayed, we suspect by early morning fog affecting the continental car

197

ferries. After hearing on the radio that two people were being sought for the kidnapping of a young woman, he reported the incident, but by the time the police arrived, they had been picked up in a Jaguar car, of which he noted the number. The same car is standing now in your stable-yard.''

''But this is nonsense. That Jag belongs to my brother-in-law.''

''Quite, sir. The gentleman was seen to arrive here around noon with two passengers, whom you and he took into the house. And I do have a search-warrant.''

''There's obviously some mistake, Inspector, but the house is full of paying customers that I don't know from Adam, there may be all sorts of crooked characters among them, so do go ahead and search.''

''Thank you. And we'd like you to accompany us, please.''

''Of course. In a moment. I have to attend to something first.''

He had hoped to find Nick and tell him to get the Vincents out of the attic and smuggle them out masquerading as sightseers. But the Inspector was not allowing that. ''I'd rather you stayed with us, sir, and attended to the other matter afterwards.''

The police began their search by clearing the house of media people and sightseers. The detective constable who had seen the Jaguar arrive, and therefore knew the Vincents by sight, was posted to make sure they did not escape among the sightseers as they filed past him out of the front door. After investigating the possible hiding places in the public rooms, the search-party moved on to the private part of the house. Alastair hoped they would not notice the locked door at the bottom of the stair leading to the attic, and wondered what he would say if they did.

Nick Martens had seen the police arrive. He had no idea what they wanted but seeing them there was enough. He made straight for the Jaguar to dash for freedom.

The exit from the stable-yard was clear, but a crowd of media people and sightseers blocked his way past the front of the house. Hooting furiously, he made the crowd part to let him through, and imagined for a moment that he saw the unspeakable Mrs. Grant among them. A police constable with his hand up loomed in front of the radiator. For a few mad seconds he thought of running him over. But the crowd had closed in again around the car, and a police vehicle had moved to block his escape. He halted, and the constable came to the driver's door.

"Just where d'you think you're going, sir?" he asked.

Outside the locked door leading to the attic, Alastair Rendle told the police that it had been locked when he took over the house at his great-aunt's death, and no key to it had ever been found.

"In that case we'll have to break it open, won't we sir?"

A blessed diversion occurred before this could be done. Cries of alarm and horror floated up from the crowd far below in the front drive. Alastair threw up the nearest window and saw a mass of upturned faces filled with dismay. The Inspector craned out too and said: "Crikey, there must be someone on the roof!"

Caged in the attic, Paula decided that the time had come to put her plan into operation. Jimmy had fallen into a fitful, exhausted sleep, and the confused noise of a crowd floated up from the gravel sweep in front of the house, suggesting that her performance would have a sizable audience. She crept along to the far end of the range of box-like attic rooms, opened the cobwebby window and climbed out.

The window, set in the sloping roof, opened into a gutter, hidden from below by the cornice at the top of the Georgian facade. But the parapet formed by the cornice was only a foot above the gutter. She felt giddy as she stood in it looking down, and had to lean back against the sloping roof and shut her eyes.

"Help!" she shouted. "Help me."

People below looked up. Someone, mistaking the situation ludicrously, shouted "don't jump!"

She tried to explain that she had no intention of jumping, but the hubbub from below drowned her voice. It also alerted Jimmy. He too had climbed out of a window, and was sidling along the gutter towards her.

"Paula, for pete's sake!" he shouted as he drew nearer.

What did he intend to do? Pull her back into the attic? It was too late for that, the secret was out.

Jimmy, who had a bad head for heights, edged his way slowly towards her.

"Don't go any nearer, or she'll jump," shouted an idiotic voice from below.

If she did it would be good riddance, Jimmy thought confusedly. She was the one who had caused all the trouble, with her silenced and out of the way he could come to an arrangement with Rendle and Martens and get away somehow to Spain.

As the next thought came into his head, Paula saw from his eyes what it was. He would pretend to be rescuing her, and push her over the edge.

"Don't go any nearer," warned a police voice through a megaphone from below.

If safety depends on pretending to be threatening suicide, so be it, Paula thought, and sat down on the parapet with her legs dangling over the void. A sigh of horror came from the upturned faces below.

A blast of obscene language came from Jimmy, five yards away along the roof. He had never loved her, he said, and wished he had never met her. She listened, but found that she did not care. Down below the crowd had fallen silent, hungry for the next development.

Crashing noises inside the window suggested that the door leading to the attic was being broken down. Footsteps inside pounded along the floorboards, a head popped out of the nearest window, and a coaxing voice said: "Now don't do anything silly, madam, will you?"

She burst into hectic laughter. "I've no intention of jumping, if that's what you mean. Are you a policeman?"

"Yes, madam."

"In that case, I want to make a statement."

"Very well, madam, but may I suggest that you come inside?"

Down in the front drive, the media were making frantic efforts to interpret a series of dramatic but seemingly unrelated events.

"Come away," said Celia to Dr. Petroni. "We don't want to get mixed up in this."

"But you must explain your discoveries. See, even the police are confused."

"No. Let's go. Publicity's the last thing I want."

"But there are certain things about the provenance of the satyr which must be said," insisted Petroni.

"Then I shall drive you to Bicester police station and you can tell them about it there. I might do a bit of explaining too, but if you start talking to this rabble of media I shall drive off and leave you to find your own way back to Italy."

"Why do you so dislike the idea of publicity?" he asked.

She thought for some time before she answered. "I suppose because I'm not proud of what I've done. Someone has to make sure that murder doesn't go unpunished, but I'd rather people didn't know it was me."

"Thanks to you, the Marchese Morandi, who owns the Villa Salvadori, has recovered his property. He will be very grateful to you, and I am sure that the Italian Government will wish to make some recognition of your services."

"Oh dear, I hope not," Celia murmured. "If there's any suggestion of that, do please squash it flat."

At Celia's suggestion the police checked the contents of the gunroom at Baddeley Court. All the guns registered with the police were present and correct, including three sporting rifles. In due course, Italian ballistics experts established that one of these had fired the bullets which killed the Prices, and it was evidence to this effect during the extradition proceedings which clinched the matter and led to Alastair Rendle's trial and conviction for murder in an Italian court. He refused throughout the trial to name the accomplices who had been with him in the helicopter, and said what he could to ensure that Nick Martens got off very lightly. No one suspected that this was part of a bargain negotiated by Nick, who threatened otherwise to reveal that Alastair was standing trial for a murder committed by his younger son.

Baddeley Court had to be sold, and is now the regional headquarters of an insurance company. Both Rendle boys are doing well in the services, and their mother, who is a first-class cook, has started a small catering business.

The Vincents were convicted in an English court of causing a public mischief and wasting police time, but received a suspended sentence. They have invested their ill-gotten gains in a boarding-house at Ramsgate, with a specialist clientele of handicapped children and adults. Jimmy is still around, largely because Paula controls the purse-strings.

Shortly after Alastair Rendle's arrest, Celia received an ecstatic letter from Paolo Benedetti. Thanks to her, Ciampi had cleared him of any suspicion of involvement in the affair at the Villa Salvadori. His girlfriend had landed a well-paid job, and would support him while he studied law, thus escaping from the antique trade. Eventually, no doubt, they would get married.

Jane and Celia remain close friends, but have to meet furtively. Her parents have separated, and a divorce is pending. Colonel Armstrong has made it fairly clear that he would welcome Celia as a replacement for his tiresome wife, an idea which Celia has done her best to discourage.

In due course the Marchese Morandi presented himself at Archerscroft to offer Celia his formal thanks for her part in bringing about the recovery of his satyr. He was a small man, and brought with him a flat parcel almost as tall as himself, which proved to contain a large and imposing oil-painting.

''With my compliments and very warm thanks,'' he said. ''And I hope you will think the subject-matter appropriate to your circumstances.''

It was a magnificent flower-piece by the seventeenth-century Neapolitan artist Giuseppe Recco. Celia hung it in the place of honor over her fireplace, and told enquirers that it had been left to her by a great-aunt.

ABOUT THE AUTHOR

John Sherwood lives in Kent, England.